THE FIREFLY
OF FRANCE

MARION POLK ANGELLOTTI

1st WORLD
LIBRARY
Literary Society

The Firefly of France

Marion Polk Angellotti

© 1st World Library – Literary Society, 2004
PO Box 2211
Fairfield, IA 52556
www.1stworldlibrary.org
First Edition

LCCN: 2004195344

Softcover ISBN: 1-4218-0178-7
Hardcover ISBN: 1-4218-0078-0
eBook ISBN: 1-4218-0278-3

Purchase *"The Firefly of France"*
as a traditional bound book at:
www.1stWorldLibrary.org/purchase.asp?ISBN=1-4218-0178-7

1st World Library Literary Society is a nonprofit
organization dedicated to promoting literacy by:

- Creating a free internet library accessible from any
  computer worldwide.
- Hosting writing competitions and offering book
  publishing scholarships.

Readers interested in supporting literacy
through sponsorship, donations or
membership please contact:
literacy@1stworldlibrary.org
Check us out at: www.1stworldlibrary.ORG
and start downloading free ebooks today.

The Firefly of France
contributed by Tim, Ed & Rodney
in support of
1st World Library Literary Society

CHAPTER I

ALARUMS AND EXCURSIONS

The restaurant of the Hotel St. Ives seems, as I look back on it, an odd spot to have served as stage wings for a melodrama, pure and simple. Yet a melodrama did begin there. No other word fits the case. The inns of the Middle Ages, which, I believe, reeked with trap-doors and cutthroats, pistols and poisoned daggers, offered nothing weirder than my experience, with its first scene set beneath this roof. The food there is superperfect, every luxury surrounds you, millionaires and traveling princes are your fellow-guests. Still, sooner than pass another night there, I would sleep airily in Central Park, and if I had a friend seeking New York quarters, I would guide him toward some other place.

It was pure chance that sent me to the St. Ives for the night before my steamer sailed. Closing the doors of my apartment the previous week and bidding good-bye to the servants who maintained me there in bachelor state and comfort, I had accompanied my friend Dick Forrest on a farewell yacht cruise from which I returned to find the first two hotels of my seeking packed from cellar to roof. But the third had a free room, and I took it without the ghost of a presentiment. What would or would not have happened if I had not taken it is a thing I like to speculate on.

To begin with, I should in due course have joined an ambulance section somewhere in France. I should not have gone hobbling on crutches for a painful three months or more. I should not have in my possession four shell fragments, carefully extracted by a French surgeon from my fortunately hard head. Nor should I have lived through the dreadful moment when that British officer at Gibraltar held up those papers, neatly folded and sealed and bound with bright, inappropriately cheerful red tape, and with an icy eye demanded an explanation beyond human power to afford.

All this would have been spared me. But, on the other hand, I could not now look back to that dinner on the Turin-Paris *rapide*. I should never have seen that little, ruined French village, with guns booming in the distance and the nearer sound of water running through tall reeds and over green stones and between great mossy trees. Indeed, my life would now be, comparatively speaking, a cheerless desert, because I should never have met the most beautiful - Well, all clouds have silver linings; some have golden ones with rainbow edges. No; I am not sorry I stopped at the St. Ives; not in the least!

At any rate, there I was at eight o'clock of a Wednesday evening in a restaurant full of the usual lights and buzz and glitter, among women in soft-hued gowns, and men in their hideous substitute for the same. Across the table sat my one-time guardian, dear old Peter Dunstan, - Dunny to me since the night when I first came to him, a very tearful, lonesome, small boy whose loneliness went away forever with his welcoming hug, - just arrived from home in Washington to eat a farewell dinner with me and to impress upon me for the hundredth time that I had better not go.

"It's a wild-goose chase," he snapped, attacking his entree savagely. Heaven knows it was to prove so, even wilder than his dreams could paint; but if there were geese in it, myself included, there was also to be a swan.

"You don't really mean that, Dunny," I said firmly, continuing my dinner. It was a good dinner; we had consulted over each item from cocktails to liqueurs, and we are both distinctly fussy about food.

"I do mean it!" insisted my guardian. Dunny has the biggest heart in the world, with a cayenne layer over it, and this layer is always thickest when I am bound for distant parts. "I mean every word of it, I tell you, Dev." Dev, like Dunny, is a misnomer; my name is Devereux - Devereux Bayne. "Don't you risk your bones enough with the confounded games you play? What's the use of hunting shells and shrapnel like a hero in a movie reel? We're not in this war yet, though we soon will be, praise the Lord! And till we are, I believe in neutrality - upon my soul I do."

"Here's news, then!" I exclaimed. "I never heard of it before. Well, your new life begins too late, Dunny. You brought me up the other way. The modern system, you know, makes the parent or guardian responsible for the child. So thank yourself for my unneutral nature and for the war medals I'm going to win!"

Muttering something about impertinence, he veered to another tack.

"If you must do it," he croaked, "why sail for Naples instead of for Bordeaux? The Mediterranean is full of those pirate fellows. You read the papers - the head-lines anyway; you know it as well as I. It's suicide, no less! Those Huns sank the *San Pietro* last week. I say, young man, are you listening? Do you hear what I'm telling you?"

It was true that my gaze had wandered near the close of his harangue. I like to look at my guardian; the fine old chap, with his height and straightness, his bright blue eyes and proud silver head, is a sight for sore eyes, as they say. But just then I had glimpsed something that was even better worth seeing. I am not impressionable, but I must confess that I was impressed by this girl.

She sat far down the room from me. Only her back was visible and a somewhat blurred side-view reflected in the mirror on the wall. Even so much was, however, more than welcome, including as it did a smooth white neck, a small shell-like ear, and a mass of warm, crinkly, red-brown hair. She wore a rose-colored gown, I noticed, cut low, with a string of pearls; and her sole escort was a staid, elderly, precise being, rather of the trusted family-lawyer type.

"I haven't missed a word, Dunny," I assured my vis-a-vis. "I was just wondering if Huns and pirates had quite a neutral sound. You know I have to go via Rome to spend a week with Jack Herriott. He has been pestering me for a good two years - ever since he's been secretary there."

Grumbling unintelligible things, my guardian sampled his Chablis; and I, crumbling bread, lazily wishing I

Marion Polk Angellotti

could get a front view of the girl in rose-color, filled the pause by rambling on.

"Duty calls me," I declared. "You see, I was born in France. Shabby treatment on my parents' part I've always thought it; if they had hurried home before the event I might have been President and declared war here instead of hunting one across the seas. In that case, Dunny, I should have heeded your plea and stayed; but since I'm ineligible for chief executive, why linger on this side?"

He scowled blackly.

"I'll tell you what it is, my boy," he accused, with lifted forefinger. "You like to pose - that's what is the matter with you! You like to act stolid, matter-of-fact, correct; you want to sit in your ambulance and smoke cigarettes indifferently and raise your eyebrows superciliously when shrapnel bursts round. And it's all very well now; it looks picturesque; it looks good form, very. But how old are you, eh, Dev? Twenty-eight is it? Twenty-nine?"

"You should know - none better - that I am thirty," I responded. "Haven't you remembered each anniversary since I was five, beginning with a hobby-horse and working up through knives and rifles and ponies to the latest thing in cars?"

Dunny lowered his accusing finger and tapped it on the cloth.

"Thirty," he repeated fatefully. "All right, Dev. Strong and fit as an ox, and a crack polo-player and a fair shot and boxer and not bad with boats and cars and horses and pretty well off, too. So when you look bored, it's picturesque; but wait! Wait ten years, till you take on flesh, and the doctor puts you on diet, and you stop hunting chances to kill yourself, but play golf like me. Then, my boy, when you look stolid you won't be romantic. You'll be stodgy, my boy. That's what you'll be!"

Of all words in the dictionary there is surely none worse than this one. The suggestions of stodginess are appalling, including, even at best, hints of overweight, general uninterestingness, and a disposition to sit at home in smoking-jacket and slippers after one's evening meal. As my guardian suggested, my first youth was over. I held up both my hands in token that I asked for grace.

"*Kamerad*!" I begged pathetically. "Come, Dunny, let's be sociable. After all, you know, it's my last evening; and if you call me such names, you will be sorry when I am gone. By the way, speaking of Huns - it was you, the neutral, who mentioned them, - does it strike you there are quite a few of them on the staff of this hotel? I hope they won't poison me. Look at the head waiter, look at half the waiters round, and see that blond-haired, blue-eyed menial. Do you think he saw his first daylight in these United States?"

The menial in question was a uniformed bellboy winding in and out among tables and paging some elusive guest. As he approached, his chant grew plainer.

"Mr. Bayne," he was droning. "Room four hundred and three."

I raised a hand in summons, and he paused beside my seat.

"Telephone call for you, sir," he informed me.

With a word to my guardian, I pushed my chair back and crossed the room. But at the door I found my path barred by the *maitre d'hotel*, who, at the sight of my progress, had sprung forward, like an arrow from a bow.

"Excuse me, sir. You're not leaving, are you?" The man was actually breathing hard. Deferential as his bearing was, I saw no cause for the inquiry, and with some amusement and more annoyance, I wondered if he suspected me of slipping out to evade my bill.

"No," I said, staring him up and down; "I'm not!" I passed down the hall to the entrance of the telephone booths. Glancing back, I could see him still standing there gazing after me; his face, I thought, wore a relieved expression as he saw whither I was bound.

The queer incident left my mind as I secluded myself, got my connection, and heard across the wire the indignant accents of Dick Forrest, my former college chum. Upon leaving his yacht that morning, I had promised him a certain power of attorney - Dick is a lawyer and is called a good one, though I can never quite credit it - and he now demanded in unjudicial heat why it had not been sent round.

"Good heavens, man," I cut in remorsefully, "I forgot it! The thing is in my room now. Where are you? That's all right. You'll have it by messenger within ten minutes." Hastily rehooking the receiver, I bolted from my booth.

In the restaurant door against a background of paneled walls the *maitre d'hotel* still stood, as if watching for my return. I sprang into an elevator just about to start its ascent, and saw his mouth fall open and his feet bring him several quick steps forward.

"The man is crazy," I told myself with conviction as I shot up four stories in as many seconds and was deposited in my hall.

There was no one at the desk where the floor clerk usually kept vigil, gossiping affably with such employees as passed. The place seemed deserted; no doubt all the guests were downstairs. Treading lightly on the thick carpet, I went down the hall to Room four hundred and three, and found the door ajar and a light visible inside.

My bed, I supposed, was being turned down. I swung the door open, and halted in my tracks. With his back to me, bent over a wide-open trunk that I had left locked, was a man.

Stepping inside, I closed the door quietly, meanwhile scrutinizing my unconscious visitor from head to foot. He wore no hotel insignia - was neither porter, waiter, nor valet.

"Well, how about it? Anything there suit you?" I inquired affably, with my back against the door.

Exclaiming gutturally, he whisked about and faced me where I stood quite prepared for a rough-and-tumble. Instead of a typical housebreaker of fiction, I saw a

Marion Polk Angellotti

pale, rabbit-like, decent-appearing little soul. He was neatly dressed; he seemed unarmed save for a great ring of assorted keys; and his manner was as propitiatory and mild-eyed as that of any mouse. There must be some mistake. He was some sober mechanic, not a robber. But on the other hand, he looked ready to faint with fright.

"*Mein Gott!*" he murmured in a sort of fishlike gasp.

This illuminating remark was my first clue.

"Ah! *Mein Herr* is German?" I inquired, not stirring from my place.

The demand wrought an instant change in him - he drew himself up, perhaps to five feet five.

"Vat you got against the Germans?" he asked me, almost with menace. It was the voice of a fanatic intoning "Die Wacht am Rhein" - of a zealot speaking for the whole embattled *Vaterland*.

The situation was becoming farcical.

"Nothing in the world, I assure you," I replied. "They are a simple, kindly people. They are musical. They have given the world Schiller, Goethe, the famous *Kultur*, and a new conception of the possibilities of war. But I think they should have kept out of Belgium, and I feel the same way about my room - and don't you try to pull a pistol or I may feel more strongly still."

"I ain't got no pistol, *nein*," declared my visitor, sulkily. His resentment had already left him; he had shrunk back to five feet three.

"Well, I have, but I'll worry along without it," I remarked, with a glance at the nearest bag. As targets, I don't regard my fellow-creatures with great enthusiasm and, moreover, I could easily have made two of this mousy champion of a warlike race. Illogically, I was feeling that to bully him was sheer brutality. Besides this, my dinner was not being improved by the delay.

"Look here," I said amiably, "I can't see that you've taken anything. Speak up lively now; I'll give you just one chance. If you care to tell me how you got through a locked door and what you were after, I'll let you go. I'm off to the firing line, and it may bring me luck!"

Hope glimmered in his eyes. In broken English, with a childlike ingenuousness of demeanor, he informed me that he was a first-class locksmith - first-glass he called it - who had been sent by the management to open a reluctant trunk. He had entered my room, I was led to infer, by a mistake.

"I go now, *ja*?" he concluded, as postscript to the likely tale.

"The devil you do! Do you take me for an utter fool?" I asked, excusably nettled, and stepping to the telephone, I took the receiver from its hook.

"Give me the manager's office, please," I requested, watching my visitor. "Is this the manager? This is Mr. Bayne speaking, Room four hundred and three. I've found a man investigating my trunk - a foreigner, a German." An exclamation from the manager, and from the listening telephone-girl a shriek! "Yes; I have him. Yes; of course I can hold him. Send up your house detective and be quick! My dinner is spoiling -"

The receiver dropped from my hand and clattered against the wall. The little German, suddenly galvanized, had leaped away from the trunk, not toward me and the door beyond me, but toward the electric switch. His fingers found and turned it, plunging the room into the darkness of the grave. Taken unaware, I barred his path to the hall, only to hear him fling up the window across the room. Against the faint square of light thus revealed, I saw him hang poised a moment. Then with a desperate noise, a moan of mixed resolve and terror, he disappeared.

CHAPTER II

DEUTSCHLAND UBER ALLES

Standing there staring after him, I felt like a murderer of the deepest dye. It is one thing to hand over to the police their natural prey, a thief taken red-handed, but quite another, and a much more harrowing one, to have him slip through your fingers, precipitate himself into mid-air, and drop four stories to the pavement, scattering his brains far and wide. There was not a vestige of hope for the poor wretch.

Unnerved, I groped to the window and peered downward for his remains. My first glance proved my regrets to be superfluous. Beneath my window, which, owing to the crowded condition of the hotel, opened on a side street, a fire-escape descended jaggedly; and upon it, just out of arm's reach, my recent guest clung and wobbled, struggling with an attack of natural vertigo before proceeding toward the earth.

By this time my rage was such that I would have followed that little thief almost anywhere. It was not the dizziness of the yawning void that stayed me. I should have climbed the Matterhorn with all cheerfulness to catch him at the top. But sundry visions of the figure I would cut, the crowd that might gather, and the probable ragging in the morning papers, were too much for me, and I sorrowfully admitted that the game was not worth the price.

The little man's nerves, meanwhile, seemed to be steadying. Feeling each step, he began cautiously to work his way down. To my wrath he even looked up at me and indulged in a grimace - but his triumph was ill-timed, for at that very instant I beheld, strolling along the street below, humming and swinging his night-stick, as leisurely, complacent, and stalwart a representative of the law as one could wish to see.

"Hi, there! Officer!" I shouted lustily. My hail, if not my words, reached him; he glanced up, saw the figure on the ladder, and was seized instantaneously with the spirit of the chase.

Yelling something reassuring, the gist of which escaped me, he constituted himself a reception committee of one and started for the ladder's foot. But our doughty Teuton was a resourceful person. Roused to the urgency of his plight, he looked wildly up at me, down at the officer, and, hastily pushing up the nearest window, hoisted himself across its sill, and again took refuge in the St. Ives Hotel.

With a bellow of rage, the policeman dashed toward the porte-cochere, while I ducked back into the room, rapidly revolving my chances of cutting off the man's retreat below. If the system of numbering was the same on every floor, my thief must, of course, emerge from Room 303. But this similarity was problematical, and to invade apartments at random, disturbing women at their opera toilets and maybe even waking babies, was too desperate a shift to try.

It reminded me to wait with what patience I could summon for the house detective. And where was he, by the way? I had turned in my alarm a good five minutes before.

In an unenviable humor I stumbled across the room, tripping and barking my shins over various malignant hassocks, tables, and chairs. Finding the switch at last, I flooded the room with light, and saw myself in the mirror, with tie and coat askew.

"Now," I muttered, straightening them viciously, "we'll see what he took away." But the trunk seemed undisturbed when I examined it, and my various bags and suitcases were securely locked. I had found Forrest's power of attorney and was storing it in my pocket when voices rose outside.

A group of four was approaching, comprised of a spruce, dress-coated manager; a short thick-set, broad-faced man who was doubtless the long-overdue detective; a professional-appearing gentleman with a black bag, obviously the house-physician; and the policeman that I had summoned from his stroll below. The latter, in an excited brogue, was recounting his late vision of the thief, "hangin' between hivin and earth, no less," while the detective scornfully accused him of having been asleep or jingled, on the ground of my late telephone to the effect that I was holding the man.

The manager, as was natural, took the initiative, bustling past me into my room and peering eagerly around.

"I needn't say, Mr. Bayne," he orated fluently, "how sorry I am that this has happened - especially beneath our roof. It is our first case, I assure you, of anything so regrettable. If it gets into the papers it won't do us any good. Now the important thing is to take the fellow out by the rear without courting notice. Why, where is he?" he asked hopefully. "Surely he isn't gone?"

"Sure, and didn't I tell ye? 'Tis without eyes ye think me!" The policeman was resentful, and so, to tell the truth, was I. The whole maddening affair seemed bent on turning to farce at every angle; the doctor, as a final straw, had just offered *sotto voce* to mix me a soothing draft!

"Gone! Of course he's gone, man!" I exclaimed with some natural temper. "Did you expect him to sit here waiting all this time? What on earth have you been doing - reading the papers - playing bridge? A dozen thieves could have escaped since I telephoned downstairs!"

"But you said," he murmured, apparently dazed, "that you could hold him." A tactless remark, which failed to assuage my wrath!

"So I could," I responded savagely. "But I didn't expect him to turn into a conjuring trick, which is what he did. He went out that window head foremost, down the ladder, and into the room below. Let's be after him - though we stand as much chance of catching him as we do of finding the King of England!" and I turned toward the doorway, where the manager, the doctor and the detective were massed.

The manager put his hand upon my arm. I looked down at it with raised eyebrows, and he took it away.

"Excuse me, sir," he said, adopting a manner of appeal, "but if you'll reflect for a moment you'll see how it is, I know. People don't care for houses where burglars fly in and out of windows; it makes them nervous; you wouldn't believe how easily a hotel can get a bad name and lose its clientele. Besides, from what you tell me, the fellow must be well away by this time. You'd do me a favor - a big one - by dropping the matter here."

"Well, I won't!" I snapped indignantly. "I'll see it through - or start something still livelier. Are you coming down with me to investigate the room beneath us or do you want me to ring up police headquarters and find out why?"

In the hall the policeman looked at me across the intervening heads and dropped one slow, approving eyelid. "If the gintleman says so - " he remarked in heavy tones fraught with meaning, and fixed a cold, blue, appraising gaze on the detective, who thereupon yielded with unexpectedly good grace.

"Aw, what's eating you?" was his amiable demand. "Sure, we was going right down there anyhow - soon's we found out how the land lay up here."

The five of us took the elevator to the lower floor. An unfriendly atmosphere surrounded me. I was held a hotel wrecker without reason. We found the corridor empty, the floor desk abandoned - a state of things rather strikingly the duplicate of that reigning over-head - and in due course paused before Room 303, where the manager, figuratively speaking, washed his hands of the affair.

"Here is the room, Mr. Bayne, for which you ask." If I

would persist in my nefarious course, added his tone.

The detective, obeying the hypnotic eye of the policeman, knocked. There was silence. The bluecoat, my one ally, was crouching for a spring. Then light steps crossed the room, and the door was opened. There stood a girl, - a most attractive girl, the girl that I had seen downstairs. Straight and slender, spiritedly gracious in bearing, with gray eyes questioning us from beneath lashes of crinkly black, she was a radiant figure as she stood facing us, with a coat of bright-blue velvet thrown over her rosy gown.

"Beg pardon, miss," said the policeman, brightly, "this gintleman's been robbed."

As her eyebrows went up a fraction, I could have murdered him, for how else could she read his statement save that I took her for the thief?

"I am very sorry," I explained, bowing formally, "to disturb you. We are hunting a thief who took French leave by my fire-escape. I must have been mistaken - I thought that he dodged in again by this window. You have not seen or heard anything of him, of course?"

"No, I haven't. But then, I just this instant came up from dinner," she replied. Her low, contralto tones, quite impersonal, were yet delightful; I could have stood there talking burglars with her till dawn. "Do you wish to come in and make sure that he is not in hiding?" With a half smile for which I didn't blame her, she moved a step aside.

"Certainly not!" I said firmly, ignoring a nudge from the policeman. "He left before you came - there was ample time. It is not of the least consequence, anyhow. Again I beg your pardon." As she inclined her head, I bowed, and closed the door.

"I trust Mr. Bayne, that you are satisfied at last." This was the St. Ives manager, and I did not like his tone.

"I am satisfied of several things," I retorted sharply, "but before I share them with you, will you kindly tell me your name?"

"My name is Ritter," he said with dignity. "I confess I fail to see what bearing -"

"Call it curiosity," I interrupted. "Doctor, favor me with yours."

The doctor peered at me over his glasses, hesitated, and then revealed his patronym. It was Swanburger, he informed me.

"But, my dear sir, what on earth -"

"Merely," said I, with conviction, "that this isn't an Allies' night. It is *Deutschland uber Alles*; the stars are fighting for the Teuton race. Now, let's hear how you were christened," I added, turning to the house detective, who looked even less sunny than before if that could be.

"See here, whatcher giving us?" snarled that somewhat unpolished worthy. "My name's Zeitfeld; but I was born in this country, don't you forget it, same as you."

"A great American personality," I remarked dreamily, "has declared that in the hyphenate lies the chief menace to the United States. And what's your name?" I asked the representative of law and order. "Is it Schmidt?"

"No, sir," he responded, grinning; "it's O'Reilly, sorr."

"Thank heaven for that! You've saved my reason," I assured him as I leaned against the wall and scanned the Germanic hordes.

"Mr. Ritter," said I, addressing that gentleman coldly, "when I am next in New York I don't think I shall stop with you. The atmosphere here is too hectic; you answer calls for help too slowly - calls, at least, in which a guest indiscreetly tells you that he has caught a German thief. It looks extremely queer, gentlemen. And there are some other points as well -"

But there I paused. I lacked the necessary conviction. After all I was the average citizen, with the average incredulity of the far-fetched, the melodramatic, the absurd. To connect the head waiter's panic at my departure with the episode in my room, to declare that the floor clerks had been called from their posts for a set purpose, and the halls deliberately cleared for the thief, were flights of fancy that were beyond me. The more fool I!

By the time I saw the last of the adventure I began that night - it was all written in the nth power, and introduced in more or less important roles the most charming girl in the world, the most spectacular hero of France, the cleverest secret-service agent in the pay of the fatherland, and I sometimes ruefully suspected, the biggest imbecile of the United States in the person of myself - I knew better than to call any idea impossible simply because it might sound wild. But at the moment my education was in its initial stages, and turning with a shrug from three scowling faces, I led my friendly bluecoat a little aside.

"I've no more time to-night to spend thief-catching, Officer," I told him. I had just recalled my dinner, now utterly ruined, and Dunny, probably at this instant cracking walnuts as fiercely as if each one were the kaiser's head. "But I'm an amateur in these affairs, and you are a master. Before I go, as man to man, what the dickens do you make of this?"

Flattered, he looked profound.

"I'm thinking, sorr," he gave judgment, "ye had the rights of it. Seein' as how th' thafe is German, ye'll not set eyes on him more - for divil a wan here but's of that counthry, and they stick together something fierce!"

"Well," I admitted, "our thoughts run parallel. Here is something to drink confusion to them all. And, O'Reilly, I am glad I'm going to sail to-morrow. I'd rather live on a sea full of submarines than in this hotel, wouldn't you?"

Touching his forehead, he assented, and wished me good-night and a good journey; part of his hope went unfulfilled, by the way. That ocean voyage of mine was to take rank, in part at least, as a first-class nightmare. The Central powers could scarcely have improved on it by torpedoing us in mid-ocean or by speeding us upon our trip with a cargo of clock-work bombs.

CHAPTER III

ON THE RE D'ITALIA

The sailing of the *Re d'Italia* was scheduled for 3 P.M. promptly, but being well acquainted with the ways of steamers at most times, above all in these piping times of war, it was not until an hour later than I left the St. Ives, where the manager, by the way, did not appear to bid me farewell.

The thermometer had been falling, and the day was crisp and snappy, with a light powdering of snow underfoot and a blue tang and sparkle in the air. Dunny accompanied me in the taxicab, but was less talkative than usual. Indeed, he spoke only two or three times between the hotel and the pier.

"I say, Dev," was his first contribution to the conversation, "d' you remember it was at a dock that you and I first met? It was night, blacker than Tophet, and raining, and you came ashore wet as a rag. You were the lonesomest, chilliest, most forlorn little tike I ever saw; but, by the eternal, you were trying not to cry!"

"Lonesome? I rather think so!" I echoed with conviction. "Wynne and his wife brought me over; he played poker all the way, and she read novels in her berth. And I heard every one say that I was an orphan, and it was very, very sad. Well, I was never lonely after that, Dunny." My hand met his half-way.

The next time that he broke silence was upon the ferry, when he urged on me a fat wallet stuffed with plutocratic-looking notes.

"In case anything should happen," ran his muttered explanation. I have never needed Dunny's money, - his affection is another matter, - but he can spare it, and this time I took it because I saw he wanted me to.

As we approached the Jersey City piers, he seemed to shrink and grow tired, to take on a good ten years beyond his hale and hearty age. With every glance I stole at him a lump in my throat grew bigger, and in the end, bending forward, I laid a hand on his knee.

"Look here, Dunny," I demanded, not looking at him, "do you mean half of what you were saying last evening - or the hundredth part? After all, there'll be a chance to fight here before we're many months older. If you just say the word, old fellow, I'll be with you to-night - and hang the trip!"

But Dunny, though he wrung my hand gratefully and choked and glared out of the window, would hear of no such arrangement, repudiated it, indeed, with scorn.

"No, my boy," he declared. "I don't say it for a minute. I like your going. I wouldn't give a tinker's dam for you, whatever that is, if you didn't want to do something for those fellows over there. I won't even say to be careful, for you can't if you do your duty - only, don't you be too all-fired foolhardy, even for war medals, Dev."

"Oh, I was born to be hanged, not shot," I assured him, almost prophetically. "I'll take care of myself, and I'll write you now and then -"

"No, you won't!" he snorted, with a skepticism amply justified by the past. "And if you did, I shouldn't answer; I hate letters, always did. But you cable me once a fortnight to let me know you're living - and send an extra cable if you want anything on earth!"

The taxi, which had been crawling, came to a final halt, and a hungry horde, falling on my impedimenta, lowered them from the driver's seat.

"No, I'll not come on board, Dev," said my guardian. "I - I couldn't stand it. Good-by, my dear boy."

We clasped hands again; then I felt his arm resting on my shoulder, and flung both of mine about him in an old-time, boyish hug.

"*Au revoir*, Dunny. Back next year," I shouted cheerily as the driver threw in his clutch and the car glided on its way.

Preceded by various porters, I threaded my way at a snail's pace through the dense crowd of waiting passengers, swarthy-faced sons of Italy, apparently bound for the steerage. The great gray bulk of the *Re d'Italia* loomed before me, floating proudly at her stern the green, white, and red flag blazoned with the Savoyard shield.

"Wave while they let you," I apostrophized it, saluting.

"When we get outside the three-mile limit and stop courting notice, you'll not fly long."

At the gang-plank I was halted, and I produced my passport and exhibited the *vise* of his excellency, the Italian consul-general in New York. I strolled aboard, was assigned to Cabin D, and informed by my steward that there were in all but five first-class passengers, a piece of news that left me calm. Stodgy I may be, - it was odd how that term of Dunny's rankled, - but I confess that I find chance traveling acquaintances boring and avoid them when I can. Unlike most of my countrymen, I suppose I am not gregarious, though I dine and week-end punctiliously, send flowers and leave cards at decorous intervals, and know people all the way from New York to Tokio.

My carefully limited baggage looked lonely in my cabin; I missed the paraphernalia with which one usually begins a trip. Also, as I rummaged through two bags to find the cap I wanted, I longed for Peters, my faithful man, who could be backed to produce any desired thing at a moment's notice. When bound for Flanders or the Vosges, however, one must be a Spartan. I found what I sought at last and went on deck.

The scene, though cheerful, was not lacking in wartime features: A row of life-boats hung invitingly ready; a gun, highly dramatic in appearance, was mounted astern, with every air of meaning business should the kaiser meddle with us en route. Down below, the Italians, talking, gesticulating, showing their white teeth in flashing, boyish smiles, were being herded docilely on board, while at intervals one or another of the few promenade-deck passengers appeared.

The first of these, a shrewd-faced, nervous little man, borrowed an unneeded match of me and remarked that it was cold weather for spring. The next, a good-looking young foreigner, - a reservist, I surmised, recalled to the Italian colors in this hour of his country's need, - rather harrowed my feelings by coming on board with a family party, gray-haired father, anxious mother, slim bride-like wife, and two brothers or cousins, all making pathetic pretense at good cheer. Soon after came a third man, dark, quiet, watchful-looking, and personable enough, although his shoes were a little too gleamingly polished, his watch and chain a little too luminously golden, the color scheme of his hose and tie selected with almost too much care.

"This," I reflected resignedly, "is going to be a ghastly trip. By Jove, here comes another! Now where have I seen her before?"

The new arrival, as indicated by the pronoun, was a woman; though why one should tempt Providence by traveling on this route at this juncture, I found it hard to guess. Standing with her back to me, enveloped in a coat of sealskin with a broad collar of darker fur, well gloved, smartly shod, crowned by a fur hat with a gold cockade, she made a delightful picture as she rummaged in a bag which reposed upon a steamer-chair, and which, thus opened, revealed a profusion of gold mountings, bottles and brushes, hand-chased and initialed in an opulent way.

There was a haunting familiarity about her. She teased my memory as I strolled up the deck. Then, snapping the bag shut, she turned and straightened, and I recognized the girl to whose door my thief-chase had led me at the St. Ives.

It seemed rather a coincidence my meeting her again.

"I shouldn't mind talking to you on this trip," I reflected, mollified. "The mischief of it is you'll notice me about as much as you notice the ship's stokers. You're not the sort to scrape acquaintance, or else I miss my shot!"

I did not miss it. So much was instantly proved. As I passed her, on the mere chance that she might elect to acknowledge our encounter, I let my gaze impersonally meet hers. She started slightly. Evidently she remembered. But she turned toward the nearest door without a bow.

The dark, too-well-groomed man was emerging as she advanced. Instead of moving back, he blocked her path, looking - was it appraisingly, expectantly? - into her eyes. There was a pause while she waited rather haughtily for passage; then he effaced himself, and she disappeared.

Striking a match viciously, I lit a cigarette and strolled forward. Either the fellow had fancied that he knew her or he had behaved in a confoundedly impertinent way. The latter hypothesis seemed, on the whole, the more likely, and I felt a lively desire to drop him over the rail.

"But I don't know what a girl of your looks expects, I'm sure," I grumbled, "setting off on your travels with no chaperon and no companion and no maid! Where are your father and mother? Where are your brothers? Where's the old friend of the family who dined with you last night? If chaps who have no right to walk the same earth with you get insolent, who is going to teach them their place, and who is going to take care of you if a U-boat pops out of the sea? Oh, well, never mind. It isn't any of my business. But just the same if you need my services, I think I'll tackle the job."

Time was passing; night had fallen. Consulting my watch, I found that it was seven o'clock. I had been aboard more than two hours. An afternoon sailing, quotha! At this rate we would be lucky if we got off by dawn.

The dinner gong, a welcome diversion, summoned us below to lights and warmth. At one table the young Italian entertained his relatives, and at another the captain, a short, swart-faced, taciturn being, had grouped his officers and various officials of the steamship company at a farewell feast. The little sharp-faced passenger was throned elsewhere in lonely splendor, but when I selected a fourth table, he jumped up, crossed over and installed himself as my vis-a-vis. Passing me the salt, which I did not require, he supplied with it some personal data of which I felt no greater need. His name was McGuntrie, he announced; he was sales agent for the famous Phillipson Rifles and was being dispatched to secure a gigantic contract on the other side.

"And if inside six months you don't see three hundred thousand Italian soldiers carrying Phillipson's best," he informed me, "I'll take a back seat and let young Jim Furman, who thinks I'm a has-been and he's the one white hope, begin to draw my pay. You can't beat those rifles. When the boys get to carrying them, old Francis Joseph's ghost'll weep. Pity, ain't it, we didn't get on board by noon?" he digressed sociably. "I could've found something to do ashore the four hours I've been twiddling my thumbs here, and I guess you could too. Hardest, though, on our friends the newspaper boys. Did you know they were out there waiting to take a flashlight film? Fact. They do it nowadays every time a big liner leaves. Then if we sink, all they have to do is run it, with 'Doomed Ship Leaving New York Harbor' underneath."

To his shocked surprise I laughed at the information. My appetite was unimpaired as I pursued my meal. Trains in which others ride may telescope and steamers may take one's acquaintances to watery graves, but to normal people the chance of any catastrophe overtaking them personally must always seem gratifyingly far-fetched and vague.

"Think it's funny, do you?" my new friend reproached me. "Well, I don't; and neither did the folks who had cabins taken and who threw them up last week when they heard how the *San Pietro* went down on this same route. We're five plumb idiots - that's what we are - five crazy lunatics! I'd never have come a step, not with wild horses dragging me if it hadn't been for Jim Furman being pretty near popeyed, looking for a chance to cut me out and sail. We've got fifteen hundred reservists downstairs, and a cargo of contraband. What do you know about that as a prize for a submarine?"

"Well," I said vaingloriously. "I can swim."

My eyes were wandering, for the girl in the fur coat had entered, with the dark, watchful-eyed man - was it pure coincidence? - close behind. The steward ushered her to a table; the man followed at her heels. I dare say I glared. I know my muscles stiffened. The fellow was going to speak to her. What in blazes did he mean by stalking her in this way?

"Excuse me," he was saying, "but haven't we met before?"

The girl straightened into rigidness, looking him over. Her manner was haughty, her ruddy head poised stiffly, as she answered in a cold tone:

"No."

He was watching her keenly.

"My name's John Van Blarcom," he persisted.

Again she gave him that sweeping glance.

"You are mistaken," she said indifferently. "I have not seen you before."

He nodded curtly.

"My mistake," he admitted. "I thought I knew you," and turning from her, he sat down at the one table still unoccupied.

"So his name's Van Blarcom," whispered my ubiquitous neighbor. "And the Italian chap over there is Pietro Ricci. The steward told me so. And the captain's name is Cecchi; get it? And I know your name, too, Mr. Bayne," he added with a grin. "The steward didn't know what was taking you over, but I guess I've got your number all right. Say, ain't you a flying man or else one of the American-Ambulance boys?"

I mustered the feeble parry that I had stopped being a boy of any sort some time ago. Then lest he wring from me my age, birthplace, and the amount of my income tax, I made an end of my meal.

On deck again I wondered at my irritation, my sense of restlessness. The little salesman was not responsible, though he had fretted me like a buzzing fly. It was rather that I had taken an intense dislike to the man calling himself Van Blarcom; that the girl, despite her haughtiness, had somehow given me an impression of uneasiness - of fear almost - as she saw him approach and heard him speak; and above all, that I should have liked to flay alive the person or persons who had let her sail unaccompanied for a zone which at this moment was the danger point of the seas.

My matter-of-fact, conservatively ordered life had been given a crazy twist at the St. Ives. As an after-math of that episode I was probably scenting mysteries where there were none. Nevertheless, I wondered - though I called myself a fool for it - if any more queer things would happen before this ship on which we five bold voyagers were confined should reach the other side.

They did.

CHAPTER IV

"EXTRA"

Toward nine o'clock to my relief it became obvious that the *Re d'Italia* was really going to sail at last. The first and second whistles, sounding raucously, sent the company officials and the family of the young officer of reserves ashore. The plank was lowered; between the ship and the looming pier a thread of black water appeared and grew; a flash and an explosion indicated that the possibly doomed liner had been filmed according to schedule. *"Evviva l'Italia!"* yelled the returning braves in the steerage - a very decent set of fellows, it struck me, to leave so cheerfully their vocations of teamster, waiter, fruit vender, and the like, and go, unforced, to wear the gray-green coats of Italy, the short feathers of the mountain climbers, the bersagliere's bunch of plumes, and to stand against their hereditary foes the Austrians, up in the snowy Alps.

The details of departure were an old tale to me. As we swung farther and farther out, I turned to a newspaper, a twentieth extra probably, which I had heard a newsboy crying along the dock a little earlier, and had bribed a steward to secure. Moon and stars were lacking to-night, but the deck lights were good reading-lamps. Moving up the rail to one of them, I investigated the world's affairs.

From the first sheet the usual staring headlines leaped at me. There were the inevitable peace rumor, the double denial, the eternal bulletin of a trench taken here, a hill recaptured there. A sensational rumor was exploited to the effect that Franz von Blenheim, one of the star secret agents of the German Empire, was at present incognito at Washington, having spent the past month in putting his finger in the Mexican pie much to our disadvantage. On the last column of the page was the photograph of a distinguished-looking young man in uniform, with an announcement that promised some interest, I thought.

"War Scandal Bursts in France," "Scion of Oldest Noblesse Implicated," "Duke Mysteriously Missing," I read in the diminishing degrees of the scare-head type. Then came the picture, with a mien attractively debonair, a pleasantly smiling mouth, and a sympathetic pair of eyes, and in due course, the tale. I clutched at the flapping ends of the paper and read on:

Of all the scandals to which the present war has given birth, none has stirred France more profoundly than that implicating Jean-Herve-Marie-Olivier, Count of Druyes, Marquis of Beuil and Santenay, and Duke of Raincy-la-Tour. This young nobleman, head of a family that has played its part in French history since the days of the Northmen and the crusaders, bears in his veins the bluest blood of the old regime, and numbers among his ancestors no fewer than seven marshals and five constables of France.

A noted figure not only by his birth, his wealth, and his various historic chateaux, but also by his sporting proclivities, his daring automobile racing, his marvelous fencing, and his spectacular hunting trips, the Duke of Raincy-la-Tour has long been in addition an amateur aviator of considerable fame, and it was to the French Flying Corps that he was attached when hostilities began. Here he distinguished himself from the first by his coolness, his extraordinary resource, and his utter contempt for danger, and became one of the idols of the French army and a proverb for success and audacity, besides attaining to the rank of lieutenant, gaining, after his famous night flight across Mulhausen for bomb-dropping purposes, the affectionate sobriquet of the Firefly of France, and winning in rapid succession the military Medal, the ribbon of the Legion of Honor, and the Cross of War with palms.

According to rumor, the duke was lately intrusted with a mission of exceptional peril, involving a flight into hostile territory and the capture of certain photographs of defenses much needed for the plans of the supreme command. With his wonted brilliancy, he is said to have accomplished the errand and to have returned in safety as far as the French lines. Here, however, we enter the realm of conjecture. The duke has disappeared; the plans he bore have never reached the generalissimo; and rumor persistently declares that at some point upon his return journey he was intercepted by German agents and induced by bribes or coercion to deliver up his spoils. By one version he was later captured and summarily executed by the French; while his friends, denying this, pin their hopes to his death at the hands of the enemy, as offering the best outcome of the unsavory event.

The family of the Duke of Raincy-la-Tour has been noted in the past for its pronouncedly Royalist tendencies, the attitude of his father and grandfather toward the republic having been hostile in the extreme. It is believed that this fact may have its significance in the present episode. The occurrence is of special interest to the United States in view of the recent (Continued on Page Three)

Before proceeding, I glanced at the pictured face. The Duke of Raincy-la-tour looked back at me with cool, clear eyes, smiling half aloofly, a little scornfully, as in the presence of danger the true Frenchman is apt to smile.

"I don't think, Jean-Herve-Marie-Olivier," I reflected, "that you ever talked to the Germans except with bombs. They probably got you, poor chap, and you're lying buried somewhere while the gossips make a holiday of the fact that you don't come home. Confound 'current rumors' anyhow, and yellow papers too!"

"I beg your pardon," said a low contralto voice.

The girl in the fur coat was standing at my shoulder. I turned, lifting my cap, wondering what under heaven she could want. I was not much pleased to tell the truth; a goddess shouldn't step from her pedestal to chat with strangers. Then suddenly I recognized a distinct oddness in her air.

"Would you lend me your paper," she was asking, "for just a moment? I haven't seen one since morning; the evening editions were not out when I came on board."

Her manner was proud, spirited, gracious; she even smiled; but she was frightened. I could read it in her

Marion Polk Angellotti

slight pallor, in the quickening of her breath.

My extra! What was there in the day's news that could upset her? I was nonplussed, but of course I at once extended the sheet.

"Certainly!" I replied politely. "Pray keep it." Lifting my cap a second time, I turned to go.

Her fingers touched my arm.

"Wait! Please wait!" she was urging. There was a half-imperious, half-appealing note in her hushed voice.

I stared.

"I'm afraid," I said blankly, "that I don't quite -"

"Some one may suspect. Some one may come," urged this most astonishing young woman. "Don't you see that - that I'm trusting you to help me? Won't you stay?"

Wondering if I by any chance looked as stunned as I felt, I bowed formally, faced about, and waited, both arms on the rail. My ideas as to my companion had been revolutionized in sixty seconds. I had believed her a girl with whom I might have grown up, a girl whose brother and cousins I had probably known at college, a girl that I might have met at a friend's dinner or at the opera or on a country-club porch if I had had my luck with me. Now what was I to think her - an escaped lunatic or something more accountable and therefore worse? If I detest anything, it is the unconventional, the stagy, the mysterious. Setting my teeth, I resolved to wait until she concluded her researches; after that, politely but firmly, I would depart.

And then, beside me, the paper rustled. I heard a little gasp, a tiny low-drawn sigh. Stealing a glance down, I saw the girl's face shining whitely in the deck light. Her black lashes fringed her cheeks as her head bent backward; her eyes were as dark as the water we were slipping through. I had no idea of speaking, and yet I did speak.

"I am afraid," I heard myself saying, "that you have had bad news."

She was struggling for self-control, but her voice wavered.

"Yes," she agreed; "I am afraid I have."

"If there is anything I can do -" I was correct, but reluctant. How I would bless her if she would go away!

But obviously she did not intend to. Quite the contrary!

"There is something," she was murmuring, "that would help me very much."

There, I had done it! I was an ass of the common or garden variety, who first resolved to keep out of a queer business and then, because a girl looked bothered, plunged into it up to my ears. I succeeded in hiding my feelings, in looking wooden.

"Please tell me," I responded, "what it is."

"But - I can't explain it." Her gloved hands tightened

on the railing. "And if I ask without explaining, it will seem so - so strange."

"Doubtless," I reflected grimly. But I had to see the thing through now. "That doesn't matter at all," I assured her civilly through clenched teeth.

She came closer - so close that her fur coat brushed me, and her breath touched my cheek; her eyes, like gray stars now that they were less anxious, went to my head a little, I suppose. Oh, yes, she was lovely. Of course that was a factor. If she had been past her first youth and skimpy as to hair, and dowdy, I don't pretend that I should ever have mixed myself up in the preposterous coil.

"This paper," she whispered, holding out the sheet, "has something in it. It is not about me; it is not even true. But if it stays aboard the ship, - if some one sees it, it may make trouble. Oh, you see how it sounds; I knew you would think me mad!"

"Not in the least." What an absurd rigmarole she was uttering! Yet such was the spell of her eyes, her voice, her nearness that I merely felt like saying, "Tell me some more."

" I can't destroy it myself," she went on anxiously. "He - they - mustn't see me do anything that might lead them to - to guess. But no one will think of you, nobody will be watching you; so by and by will you weight the paper with something heavy and drop it across the rail?"

My head was whirling, but a graven image might have envied me my impassivity. I bowed. "I shall be delighted," I announced banally, "to do as you say."

Her face flushed to a warm wild-rose tint as she heard me promise it, and her red lips, parting, took on a tremulous smile.

"Thank you," she murmured in frank gratitude. "I thought - I knew you would help me!" Then she was gone.

My trance broken I woke to hear myself softly swearing. I consigned myself to my proper home, an asylum; I wished the girl at Timbuktu, Kamchatka, Land's End - anywhere except on this ship. As I had told the agent of the Phillipson Rifles, I am no boy. One can scarcely knock about the world for thirty years without gaining some of its wisdom; and of all the appropriate truisms I spared myself not one.

Resentfully I reminded myself that mysteries were suspicious, that honest people seldom had need of secrecy, that idiots who, like me, consented to act blindfold would probably repent their blindness in sackcloth and ashes before long. But what use were these sage reflections? I had given my word to her. I was in for the consequences, however unpleasant they proved.

Without further mental parley I went down to my cabin, where I routed out from among my traps a bronze paper-weight as heavy as lead. Wrapping the mysterious sheet about it, I brought the package back on deck. There was not a soul in sight; it was a propitious hour.

To right and to left the coast lights were slipping past,

making golden paths on the black water as our tug pulled us out to sea. The reservists down below were singing "*Va fuori, o stranier!*" I dropped my package overboard, watched it vanish, and turned to behold the sphinx-like Van Blarcom, sprung up as if by magic, regarding me placidly from the shelter of the smoking-room door.

CHAPTER V

MR. VAN BLARCOM. U. S. A.

For a trip that had begun with such rich promise of the unusual, my voyage on the *Re d'Italia* proved a gratifying anticlimax during its first few days. The weather was bad. We plowed forward monotonously, flagless, running between dark-gray water and a lowering, leaden sky. Screws throbbed, timbers creaked, and dishes crashed as the Gulf Stream took us, and great waves reared themselves round us like myriads of threatening Alps.

After that first night the girl kept discreetly to her stateroom. I was relieved; but I thought of her a good deal. I had little else to do. Pacing a drunken deck and smoking, I wove unsatisfactory theories, asking myself what was her need of secrecy, what the item she wanted hidden, what the errand that had made her sail on the vessel a week after the spectacular torpedoing of a sister-ship? Did she know this Van Blarcom or did she merely dread any notice? And above all, who was the man and had he been watching when I tossed that wretched extra across the rail?

I saw something of him, of course, as time went on. Naturally we four bold spirits, the ubiquitous McGuntrie, Van Blarcom, the young reservist Pietro

Ricci, - a very good sort of fellow, - and I were herded together beyond escape. Also, a foursome at bridge seemed divinely indicated by our number, and to avert a sheer paralysis of ennui we formed the habit of winning each other's money at that game.

As we played I studied Van Blarcom, but without results. It was ruffling; I should have absorbed in so much intercourse a fairly definite impression of his personality, profession, and social grade. But he was baffling; reticent, but self-assured, authoritative even, and, in a quiet way, watchful. He smoked a good cigar, mixed a good drink, seemed used to travel, but produced a coarse-grained effect, made grammatical errors, and on the whole was a person from whom, once ashore, I should flee.

At six o'clock on the seventh night out our voyage entered its second lap; all the electric lights were simultaneously extinguished as we entered the danger zone. We made a sketchy toilet by means of tapers, groped like wandering ghosts down a dim corridor, and dined by the faint rays of candles thrust into bottles and placed at intervals along the festive board. I went on deck afterward to find the ship plunging through blackness on forced draft, with port-holes shrouded and with not even a riding-light. If not in Davy Jones's locker by that time, we should reach Gibraltar the next evening; afterward we should head for Naples, a two days' trip.

The following morning found our stormy weather over. The sea through which we were speeding had a magic color, the dark, rich, Mediterranean blue. Ascending late, I saw gulls flying round us and seaweed drifting by, and Mr. McGuntrie in a state of nerves, with a life belt about him, walking wildly to and fro.

"Well, Mr. Bayne," he greeted me, "never again for mine! If I ever see the end of this trip, - if you call it a trip; I call it merry hades, - believe me, I'll sell something hereafter that I can sell on land. I'm a crackerjack of a salesman, if I do say it myself. Once I got started talking I could get a man down below to buy a hot toddy and a set of flannels - and I wish I'd gone down there and done it before I ever saw this boat."

Unmoved, I leaned on the railing and watched the blue swells break. McGuntrie took a turn or two. In the ship's library he had discovered a manual entitled "How to Swim," and he was now attempting between laments to memorize its salient points.

"The first essay is best made in water of not less than fifty degrees Fahrenheit, and not more than four feet in depth," he gabbled, and then broke off to gaze at the sea about us, chilly in temperature, and countless fathoms deep. "Oh, what's the use? What the blue blazes does it matter?" he cried hysterically. "I tell you that U-boat that sank the *San Pietro* is laying for us. In about an hour you'll see a periscope bob up out there. Then we'll send out an S.O.S., and the next thing you know we'll sink with all on board."

We had as yet escaped this doom when toward six o'clock we approached Gibraltar, running beneath a crimson sunset and between misty purple shores. On one hand lay Africa, on the other the Moorish country, both shrouded in a soft haze and edged with snowy foam. Down below the soldiers of Italy were singing.

A merchantman of belligerent nationality, our ship proudly flew its flag again. Indeed, had it failed to do so, the British patrol-boats would long since have known the reason why.

It was growing dark when I turned to find Van Blarcom at my elbow.

"I didn't see you," I commented rather shortly. I don't like people to creep up beside me like cats.

"No," he responded. "I've been waiting quite a while. I didn't want to disturb you, but the fact is I'd like a word with you, Mr. Bayne."

I eyed him with curiosity. He was inscrutable, this quiet, alert, efficient-looking man. Take, for instance, his present manner, half self-assured, half respectfully apologetic - what grade in life did it fit?

"Well, here I am," I said briefly as I struck a match.

"I've thought it over a good bit," he went on, apparently in self-justification. "I don't know how you will take it, but I'll chance it just the same. If I don't give you a hint, you don't get a square deal. That's my attitude. Did you ever hear of Franz von Blenheim, Mr. Bayne?"

"Eh?" The question seemed distinctly irrelevant - and yet where had I heard that name, not very long ago?

"The German secret-service agent. The best in the world, they say." A sort of reluctant admiration showed in Van Blarcom's face. "There isn't any one that can get him; he does what he wants, goes where he likes - the United States, England, France, Russia - and always gets away safe. You'd think he was a conjurer to read what he does sometimes. A whole country will be looking for him, and he takes some one else's passport, puts on a disguise, and good-by - he's gone! That's Franz von Blenheim. No; that's just an outline of him. And on pretty good authority, he's in Washington now."

Mr. Van Blarcom, I reflected, was surely coming out of his shell; this was quite a monologue with which he was favoring me. It was dark now; our lights were flaring. Being in a friendly port's shelter, we burned electricity to-night.

"You seem to know a whole lot about this fellow," I remarked idly in the pause.

"Yes, I do." He smiled a trifle grimly. "In fact, I once came near getting him; it would have made my fortune, too. But he slipped through my fingers at the last minute, and if I ever - You see, I'm in the secret-service myself, Mr. Bayne."

I turned to stare at him.

"The United States service?" I asked.

"Yes."

I nodded. All that had puzzled me was fairly clear in this new light. Not at all the type of the star agents, those marvelous beings who figure so romantically in fiction and on the boards, he was yet, I fancied, a good example of the ruck of his profession, those who did the every-day detective work which in such a business must be done. But - Franz von Blenheim? What was my association with the name? Then I recalled that in the extra I had read as we left harbor there had been some account of the man's activities in Mexico.

"What I wanted to say was this," Van Blarcom continued in his usual manner - the manner that I now recognized to be a subtler form of the policeman's, respectful to those he held for law-abiding, alert and watchful to detect gentry of any other kind. "This line we're traveling on now is one the spies use quite a bit. They used to go to London straight or else to Bordeaux and Paris; but the English and French got a pretty strict watch going, and now it's easier for them to slip into France through Italy, by Modane. They sail for Naples mostly, do you see? And - you won't repeat this? - it's fairly sure that when Franz von Blenheim sends his government a report of what he's done in Mexico against us, he'll send it by an agent who travels on this line and lands in Italy and then slips into Germany by way of Switzerland."

We were drifting slowly into the harbor of Gibraltar, the rock looming over us through the blackness, a gigantic mountain, a mass of tiered and serried lights. Search-lights, too, shot out like swords, focused on us, and swept us as we crept forward between dimly visible, anchored craft. The throbbing of our engines ceased. A launch chugged toward us, bringing the officers of the port. I watched, pleased with the scene, and rather taken with my companion's discourse. It was not unlike a dime novel of my youth.

"Do you mean you've been sent on this line to watch for one of Blenheim's agents?" I inquired.

"No. I'm sent for some work on the other side - and I'm not telling you what it is, either," he rejoined. "What I meant was that a man has to be careful, traveling on these ships. They watch close. They have to. Haven't you noticed that whenever two or three of us get to talking, a steward comes snooping round? Well, I suppose you wouldn't, it not being your business; but I have. We're watched all the time; and if we're wise, we'll mind our step. Take you, for instance. You're a good American, eh? And yet some spy might fool you with a cute story and get your help and maybe play you for a sucker on the other side. I saw that happen once. It was a nice young chap, and a pretty girl fooled him - got him into a peck of trouble. What you want to remember is that good spies never seem like spies."

If I looked as I felt just then, the search-light that swept me must have startled him. I could feel my face flushing, my hands clenching as I caught his drift. I swung round.

"What's this about?" I demanded sharply. But I knew.

"Well," said the secret-service man discreetly, "I saw something pretty funny the first night out, Mr. Bayne. It was safe enough with me; I can tell a gentleman from a spy; but if an officer had seen it, the thing wouldn't have been a joke. Suppose we put it this way. There's a person on board I think I know. I haven't got the goods, I'll own, but I don't often make mistakes. My advice to you, sir, is to steer clear of strangers. And if I were you, I -"

"That'll do, thanks!" I cut him short. "I can take care of myself. I don't say your motives are bad, - you may think this is a favor, - but I call it a confounded piece of meddling, and I'll trouble you to let it end."

He looked hurt and indignant.

"Now, look here," he remonstrated, "what have I done but give you a friendly hint not to get in bad? But maybe I was too vague about it; you just listen to a few facts. I'll tell you who that young lady is and who her people are and what she wants on the other side -"

"No, you won't!" I declared. My voice sounded savage. I was recalling how she had begged the extra of me, and how it had contained a full account of Franz von Blenheim, the kaiser's man. "The young lady's name and affairs are no concern of mine. If you know anything you can keep it to yourself."

As we glared at each other like two hostile catamounts, a steward relieved the tension by running toward us down the deck.

"*Signori, un momento, per piacere!*" he called as he came. The British officers were on board, he forthwith informed us, and were demanding, in accordance with the martial law now reigning at Gibraltar, a sight of each passenger and his passport before the ship should proceed.

CHAPTER VI

THUMBSCREWS

The salon of conversation, as the mirrored, gilded, and highly varnished apartment was grandiloquently termed, had been the very spot chosen for our presumably not very terrible ordeal. Things were well under way. At the desk in the corner one officer was jotting down notes as to the clearance papers and the cargo; while at a table in the foreground sat his comrade, in a lieutenant's uniform, with the captain of the *Re d'Italia* at his right, swart-faced and silent, and the list of the passengers lying before the pair.

As I entered a few moments behind Van Blarcom, I perceived that the interrogation had already run a partial course. Pietro Ricci, the reservist, had, no doubt, emerged with flying colors and now stood against the wall beside the doughty agent of the Phillipson Rifles, who had apparently satisfied his inquisitor, too. Near the door a group of stewards had clustered to watch with interest; and as I stood waiting, the girl in furs came in.

I put myself a hypothetical query.

"If a girl," I thought, "materializes from the void, asks an incriminating favor, and vanishes, does that put one on bowing terms with her when one meets her again?" Evidently it did, for she smiled brightly and graciously and bent her ruddy head. But she was pale, I noticed critically; there was apprehension in her eyes. Wasn't it odd that the prospect of a few simple questions from an officer should disconcert her when she had possessed the courage, or the foolhardiness, to sail on this line at this time?

Really I could not deny that all I had seen of her was most suspicious. For aught I knew, the secret-service man might be absolutely right. I had treated him outrageously. I owed him an apology, doubtless. But I still felt furious with him, and when she looked anxiously at those officers, I felt furious with them too.

Van Blarcom, his brief questioning ended, was turning from the table. As he passed, I made a point of smiling companionably at the girl.

"Now for the rack, the cord, and the thumbscrews," I murmured to her, making way.

The lieutenant was a tall, lean, muscular young man with a shrewd tanned face in which his eyes showed oddly blue, and he half rose, civilly enough, as the girl advanced.

"Please sit down," he said with a strong English accent. "I'll have to see your passport if you will be so good." She took it from the bag she carried, and he glanced at it perfunctorily.

"Your name is Esme Falconer?"

"Yes," she replied.

It was the name of the little Stuart princess, the daughter of Charles the First, whose quaint, coiffed, blue-gowned portrait hangs in a dark, gloomy gallery at Rome. I was subconsciously aware that I liked it despite its strangeness, the while I wondered more actively if that Paul Pry of a Van Blarcom had imparted to the ship's authorities the suspicions he had shared with me.

"You are an American, Miss Falconer? You were born in the States? You are going to Italy - and then home again?" The questions came in a reassuringly mechanical fashion; the man was doing his duty, nothing more.

"I may go also to France." Her voice was steady, but I saw that she had clenched her hands beneath the table.

I glanced at Van Blarcom, to find him listening intently, his neck thrust forward, his eyes almost protruding in his eagerness not to miss a word. But there was to be nothing more.

"That is satisfactory, Miss Falconer," announced the Englishman; with a little sigh of relief, she stood back against the wall.

"If you please," said the officer to me in another tone.

As I came forward, his eyes ran over me from head to foot. So did Captain Cecchi's; but I hardly noticed; these uniforms, these formalities, these war precautions, were like a dash of comic opera. I was not taking them seriously in the least. The Britisher gestured me toward a seat, but it seemed superfluous for so brief an interview , and I remained standing with my hands resting on a chair.

"I'll have your passport!" There was something curt in his manner. "Ah! And your name is -?"

"My name is Devereux Bayne."

"How old are you?"

"Thirty."

"Where do you live?"

"In New York and Washington." If he could be laconic, so could I.

"You were born in America?"

"No. I was born in Paris." By this time questions and answers were like the pop of rifle-shots.

"That was a long way from home. Lucky you chose the country of one of our Allies." Was this sarcasm or would-be humor? It had an unpleasant ring.

"Glad you like it," I responded, with a cold stare, "but I didn't pick it."

"Well, if you weren't born in the States, are you an American citizen?" he imperturbably pursued.

"If you'll consult my passport, you'll see that I am."

"Did either your father or your mother have any German blood?"

I could hear a slight rustle back of me among the passengers, none of whom, it was plain, had been subjected to such cross-questioning. I was growing restive, but I couldn't tell him it was not his business; of course it was.

"No; they didn't," I briefly replied.

"About your destination now." He was making notes of all my answers. "You are going to Italy, and then -"

"To France."

"Roundabout trip, rather. The Bordeaux route is safer just now and quicker, too. Why not have gone that way? And how long are you planning to stop over on this side?"

"It depends upon circumstances." What on earth ailed the fellow? He was as annoying as a mosquito or a gnat.

"I beg your pardon, but your plans seem rather at loose ends, don't they? What are you crossing for?"

"To drive an ambulance!" I answered as curtly as the words could be said.

I saw his face soften and humanize at the information. For once I had made a satisfactory response, it seemed. But on the heels of my answer there rose the voice of Mr. McGuntrie, sensational, accusing, pitched almost at a shriek.

"Look here, lieutenant," he was crying, "don't you let that fellow fool you. I asked him the first night out if he was an ambulance boy, and he denied it to me, up and down. I thought all along he was too smart, hooting like he did at submarines. Guess he knew one would pick him up all right if the rest of us did sink."

"How about that, Mr. Bayne?" asked the Englishman, his uncordial self once more.

It was maddening. One would have thought them all in league to prove me an atrocious criminal.

"Simply this," I replied with the iciness of restrained fury, "that this gentleman has been the steamer's pest ever since the night we sailed. If I had answered his questions, every one, down to the ship's cat, would have shared his knowledge within the hour. I did not deny anything; I simply did not assent. You are an officer in authority; I am answering you, though I protest strongly at your manner; but I don't tell my affairs to prying strangers because we are cooped up on the same boat."

"H'm. If I were you I would keep my temper." He regarded me thoughtfully, and then with rapier-like rapidity shot two questions at my head. "I say, Mr. Bayne, you're positive about your parents not having German blood, are you? And you are quite sure you were born in Paris, not in - well, Prussia, suppose we say?"

"What the -" I opportunely remembered the presence of Miss Esme Falconer. "What do you mean?" I substituted less sulphurously, but with a glare.

He bent forward, tapping his forefinger against the desk, and his eyes were like gimlets boring into mine.

"I mean," he enlightened me, his voice very hard of a sudden, "that a German agent is due to sail on this line, about this time, with certain papers, and that from one or two indications I'm not at all sure you are not the man."

With sudden perspicacity, I realized that he took me for an emissary of the great Blenheim. Exasperation overwhelmed me; would these farcical complications never cease?

"Good heavens, man," I exclaimed with conviction, "you are crazy! Look at me! Use your common-sense! What on earth is there about me to suggest a spy?"

"In a good spy there never is anything suggestive."

By Jove, that was the very thing the secret-service man had said!

"You admit you were born abroad. You claim to be bound for France, but you sail for Italy. And you are rather a soldier's type, tall, well set-up, good military carriage. You'd make quite a showing in a field uniform, I should say."

"In a fiddlestick!" I snapped, weary of the situation. "So would you - so would our friend the Italian reservist there. I'm an average American, free, white, and twenty-one, with strong pro-Ally sympathies and a passport in perfect shape. This is all nonsense, but of course there is something back of it. What has been your real reason for deviling me ever since I entered this room?"

The lieutenant was studying my face.

Marion Polk Angellotti

"Mr. Bayne," he said slowly, "do you care to tell me the nature of the package you threw across the rail the first night out?"

I heard a gasp from the group behind me, a squeal of joy from McGuntrie, a quick, low-drawn breath that surely came from the girl. Preternaturally cool, I thought rapidly.

"What's that you say? Package?" I repeated, trying to gain time.

"Yes, package!" said the Englishman, sharply. "And we'll dispense with pretense, please. These are wartimes, and from common prudence the Allies keep an eye on all passengers who choose to sail instead of staying at home as we prefer they should. Captain Cecchi here reports to me that one of his stewards saw you drop a small weighted object overboard. He has asked me to interrogate you, instead of doing it himself, so that you may have the chance to defend yourself in English, which he doesn't speak."

"*E vero*. It ees the truth," confirmed the captain of the *Re d'Italia* - the one remark, by the way, that he ever addressed to me.

"Well?" It was the Englishman's cold voice. "We are waiting, Mr. Bayne! What was this object you were so anxious to dispose of? A message from some confederate, too compromising to keep?"

Heretofore I had carefully avoided looking at Miss Falconer, but at this point, turning my head a trifle, I gave her a casual glance. Her eyes had blackened as they had done that night on the deck; her face had paled, and her breath was coming fast. But as I looked, her gaze fell, and her lashes wavered; and I knew that whatever came she did not mean to speak.

CHAPTER VII

THE TIGHTENING WEB

I did not, of course, want her to. I was no "Injun giver," and having once pledged my word to help her, I was prepared to keep it till all was blue or any other final shade. Still, it was not to be denied that my position looked incriminating. She might be as honest as the daylight, - I believed she was; I had to or else abandon her, - but she had managed to plunge me into a confounded mess.

Naturally I was exasperated at the net results of my piece of gallantry. I didn't care to be suspected; I wasn't anxious to have to lie. All the same, a plausible explanation, offered without delay, appeared essential. I should have wanted as much myself had I been guarding Gibraltar port.

"Well, Mr. Bayne?"

"Well!" I retorted coolly. "I was just wondering if I should answer. This is an infernal outrage, you know. You don't really think I'm a spy. What you are doing is to give me a third degree on general principles. If you'll excuse my saying so I think you ought to have more sense!"

"Oh, of course we ought to take you on trust," he agreed sardonically. "But we can't I'm afraid. The fact is, we have had an experience or two to shake our faith. The last time this steamer stopped here we caught a pair of spies who didn't look the part any more than you do; and since then we have rather stopped taking appearances as guarantees."

"All right, then," I responded. "I'll stretch a point since it is war-time. I give you my word that I threw overboard a small bronze paper-weight that was cluttering up my traps. There was nothing surreptitious about it; the whole steamer might have seen me. Do you care to take the responsibility of having me shot for that?"

"And I want to say, sir, that the gentleman is giving it to you straight." An unexpected voice addressed the lieutenant at my back. "I was standing at the door behind him that night, though he didn't know it, and I can take my oath that what he says is gospel truth."

My unlooked-for champion was Mr. John Van Blarcom. I stared at him, at a loss to know why, on the heels of our row on deck and my rejection of his friendly warning, he should perjure himself for me in so obliging a fashion. He had, I was aware, been too far off that night to know whether I had thrown away a paper-weight or a sand-bag. Moreover, the object had been swathed beyond recognition in the extra that was primarily responsible for all this fuss. "He is sorry for me," I decided. "He thinks the girl has made a fool of me." Instead of experiencing gratitude, I felt more galled and wrathful than before.

"Is that so? How close were you?" the lieutenant asked alertly. "About ten feet? You are quite sure? Well - it's all right, I suppose, then," he admitted in a very grudging tone.

"No, it isn't," I declared tartly. I was by no means satisfied with so half-hearted a vindication; nor did I care to owe my immunity to a patronizing lie on Mr. Van Blarcom's part. "You have accused me of spying. Do you think I'll let it go at that? I insist that you have my baggage brought up here and that you search it and search me."

The face of the Englishman really relaxed for once.

"That's a good idea. And it's what any honest man would want, Mr. Bayne," he approved. "Since you demand it - certainly, we'll do it," and he glanced at the captain, who promptly ordered two stewards to fetch my traps from below.

Things move rapidly on shipboard. My traveling impedimenta appeared in the salon almost before I could have uttered the potent name of Jack Robinson, had I cared to try. With cold aloofness I offered my keys, and the head steward knelt to officiate, while the crowd gaped and the second English officer abandoned his corner and his papers, standing forth to watch with the lieutenant and the captain, thus forming an intent and highly interested committee of three.

The investigation began, very thorough, slightly harrowing. I had not realized the embarrassing detail of such a search. An extended store of collars suitable for different occasions; neat and glossy piles of shirts, both dress and plain; black silk hose mountain high, and neckties as numerous as the sea sands. Noting the rapt attention that McGuntrie in particular gave to these disclosures, I felt that to deserve so inhuman a punishment my crime must have been black indeed. Shoes on their trees; articles of silk underwear; brushes, combs, gloves, cards, boxes of cigarettes, an extra flask; some light literature. And so on and so on, ad nauseam, till I grew dully apathetic, and roused only to praise Allah when we left the boxes for the trunk.

Hardened by this time, I brazenly endured the exhibition of my pajamas, not turning a hair when they were held up and shaken out before the attentive crowd. In a similar spirit I bore the examination of my coats and trousers, the rummaging of my vests, the investigation of my hats. "Courage!" I told myself. "Nothing in the world is endless." Indeed, the last garment was now being lifted, revealing nothing beneath it save a leather wallet carefully tied.

"Just look through that, will you?" I requested with chilling sarcasm. "Otherwise you may get to thinking later that I had a note for the kaiser there. In point of fact, those are simply some letters of introduction that I am taking to - " I broke off abruptly. "Good Lord deliver us!" I blankly exclaimed. "What's that?"

The lieutenant, complying with my request, had unbound the wallet and was flirting out its contents in fan-like fashion like a hand of cards. I saw the imposing army of letters presented me by Dunny, who knows everybody, headed by one to his old friend, the American ambassador to France. So far, so good. But beneath them, with a sickening sense of being in a bad dream, I beheld a thin sheaf of papers, neatly folded, bound with red tape and sealed with bright red wax, - an object which, to my certain knowledge, had no more business among my belongings than the knives and plates that the conjurer snatches from the surrounding atmosphere, or the hen which he evolves, clucking, from an erstwhile empty sleeve.

Standing there with the impersonal calm of utter helplessness, I watched the Britisher break the seal and unfold the sheets. They were thin and they were many and they were covered with closely jotted hieroglyphics, row upon row. But the sphinx-like quality of the contents afforded me no gleam of hope. If they had proclaimed as much in the plainest English printing, I could have been no surer that they were the papers of Franz von Blenheim; nor, as I learned a good while afterward, was I mistaken in the belief.

I was vaguely aware that the spectators were being ordered from the salon. Captain Cecchi's eyes were dark stilettos; the gaze of the Englishman was like a narrow flash of blue steel. He was going to say something. I waited apathetically. Then the words came, falling like icicles in the deadness of the hush.

"If you wish, sir," he stated, "to explain why you are traveling with cipher papers, Captain Cecchi and I will hear what you have to say."

CHAPTER VIII

WHAT A THIEF CAN DO

In sheer desperation I achieved a ghastly levity of demeanor.

"Please don't shoot me yet," I managed to request. "And if I sit down and think for a moment, don't take it for a confession. Any innocent man would be shocked dumb temporarily if his traps gave up such loot."

I sat down in dizzy fashion, my judges watching me. Through my mind, in a mad phantasmagoria, danced the series of events that had begun in the St. Ives restaurant and was ending so dramatically in the salon of this ship. Or perhaps the end had not yet arrived, I thought ironically. By a slight effort of imagination I could conjure up a scene of the sort rendered familiar by countless movie dramas - a lowering fortress wall, myself standing against it, scornfully waving away a bandage, and drawn up before me a highly efficient firing-squad.

To all intents and purposes I was a spy, caught red-handed; but with due respect for circumstantial evidence, I did not mean to remain one long. That part of it was too absurd. There must be a dozen ways out of it. Come! The fact that so strange an experience had befallen me in a New York hotel on the eve of my sailing could not be pure coincidence. There lay the clue to the mystery. Let me work it out.

And then, as my wits began groping, comprehension came to me - a sudden comprehension that left me stunned and dazed: The open trunk, the thief, the descent by the fire-escape, the girl's calm denial, turning us from the suspected floor. Yes, the girl! Heavens, what a blind dolt I had been! No wonder that Van Blarcom had felt moved to say a helping word for me, as for a congenital idiot not responsible for his acts!

"When you are ready - " the lieutenant was remarking. I pulled myself together as hastily as I could.

"First," I began, with all the resolution I could muster, "I want to say that I am as much at a loss as you are about this thing. I never set eyes upon those papers until this evening. Why, man alive, I insisted on the search! I asked you to examine the wallet! Do you think I did all that to establish my own guilt?"

"We'll keep to the point, please." His very politeness was ill omened. "The papers were in your baggage. Can you explain how they came there?"

"I am going to try," I answered coolly. "To begin with, I can vouch for it that they were not there two weeks ago when my man packed the trunk. That I can swear to, for I glanced through the letters before handing him the wallet; and when he had finished packing I locked the trunk and went yachting for five days."

" And your luggage ? Did it go with you?" queried

the Englishman.

"No; it didn't. It remained in the baggage-room of my apartment house; but when I landed and found hotel quarters, I had it sent to me at the St. Ives."

"So you stayed there!" He was eyeing me with ever-growing disfavor. "You didn't know, of course, that it was a nest of agents, a sort of rendezvous for hyphe-nates, and that the last spy we caught on this line had made it his headquarters in New York?"

"I did not," I replied stiffly. "But I can believe the worst of it. Now, here's what befell me there." I recounted my adventure briefly, beginning with the summons from restaurant to telephone.

It was strange how, as I talked, each detail fell into its place, how each little circumstance, formerly so mystifying, grew clear. The alarm of the *maitre d'hotel* over my sudden departure, his relief when I entered the booths, his corresponding horror when, emerging, I took the elevator for my room, puzzled me no longer. The deserted halls, the flight of the little German intruder, the determined lack of interest of the hotel management, were merely links in the chain.

I told a straight, unvarnished story with one exception. When I came to the point I couldn't bring in Miss Esme Falconer's name. I said non-committally that a lady had occupied the room where the thief took refuge; and I left it to be inferred that I had never seen her before or since.

The lieutenant heard my tale out with impassivity. "Is that all, Mr. Bayne?" he asked shortly, as I paused.

"Yes," I lied doggedly. "And if you want more, I call you insatiable. I've told you enough to satisfy any man's appetite for the abnormal, haven't I?"

"Your defense, then," he summed it up, "is that under the protection of a German management a German agent entered your room, opened your trunk, concealed these papers in it, and repacked it. You believe that, eh?"

It sounded wild enough, I acknowledged gloomily as I sat staring at the carpet with my elbows on my knees.

"You've been a pretty fool, a pretty fool, a pretty fool!" the refrain sang itself unceasingly in my ears. I was disgusted with the episode, more disgusted yet with my own role. Why was I lying, why making myself by my present silence as well as by my former density the flagrant confederate of a clever spy?

I shrugged my shoulders.

"Oh, what's the use?" I muttered. "No, of course I don't believe it, and you won't either if you are sane. It is too ridiculous. I might as well suggest that if the thief hadn't been gone when they arrived, the manager and the detective would have shanghaied me, or the house doctor drugged me with a hypodermic till the fellow could get away. Let's end all this! I'm ready to go ashore if you want to take me. In your place I know I should laugh at such a story; and I think that on general principles I should order the man who told it shot."

"Not necessarily, Mr. Bayne," was the cool response of the Englishman. "The trouble with you neutrals is that you laugh too much at German spies. We warn you sometimes, and then you grin and say that it's hysteria. But by and by you'll change your minds, as we did, and know the German secret service for what it is - the most competent thing, the most widely spread, and pretty much the most dangerous, that the world has to fight to-day."

"You don't mean," I inquired blankly, "that you believe me?"

It looks odd enough as I set it down. Ordinarily I expect my word to be accepted; but then, as a general thing I don't suddenly discover that I have been chaperoning a set of German code-dispatches across the seas.

"I mean," he corrected with truly British phlegm, "that I can't say positively your story is untrue. Here's the case: Some one - probably Franz von Blenheim - wants to send these papers home by way of Italy and Switzerland. Your hotel manager tells him you are going to sail for Naples; you are an American on your way to help the Allies; it's ten to one that nobody will suspect you and that your baggage will go through untouched. What does he do? He has the papers slipped into your wallet. Then he sends a cable to some friend in Naples about a sick aunt, or candles, or soap. And the friend translates the cable by a private code and reads that you are coming and that he is to shadow you and learn where you are stopping and loot your trunk the first night you spend ashore!"

"I don't grasp," I commented dazedly; "why they should weave such circles. Why not let one of their own agents bring over the papers?"

The lieutenant smiled a faint, cold, wintry smile.

"Spies," he informed me, "always think they are watched, and generally they're not wrong in thinking so. If they can send their documents by an innocent person, they had better. For my part, I call it a very clever scheme."

"I believe I am dreaming," I muttered. "Somebody ought to pinch me. You found those infernal things nestling among my coats and hose and trousers - and you don't think I put them there?"

"I didn't say that," he denied as unresponsively as a brazen Vishnu. "I simply say that I wouldn't care to order you shot as things stand now. But you'll remember that I have only your word that all this happened or that you are really an American or even that this passport is yours and that your name is - ah - Devereux Bayne. We'll have to know quite a bit more before we call this thing settled. How are you going to satisfy his Majesty the King?"

I plucked up spirit.

"Well," I suggested, "how will this suit you? I'll go down to my stateroom and stop there until we land in Italy; and, if you like, just to be on the safe side with such a desperado as I am, you can put a guard outside my door. But first, you'll send a sheaf of marconigrams for me in both directions. You're welcome to read them, of course, before they go. Then when we get to Naples, my friend, Mr. Herriott, will meet the steamer. He is second secretary at the United States embassy, and his identification will be sufficient, I suppose. Anyhow, if it isn't, I dare say the ambassador will say a word for me. I have known him for years, though not so well."

"That would be quite sufficient as to identification." He stressed the last word significantly, and I thanked heaven for Dunny and the forces which I knew that rather important old personage could set to work.

"Also," I continued coolly, "there will be various cablegrams from United States officials awaiting us, which will convince you, I hope, that I am not likely to be a spy. There will be a statement from the friend who dined with me at the St. Ives. There will be the declaration of the policeman who saw the German climb down the fire-escape and bolt into the room beneath." "And hang the expense!" I added inwardly, computing cable rates, but assuming a lordly indifference to them which only a multimillionaire could really feel.

The Englishman and the captain consulted a moment. Then the former spoke:

"That will be satisfactory, sir, to Captain Cecchi and to me. Write out your cables, if you please. They shall be sent. And I say, Mr. Bayne, - I hope you drive that ambulance. I'm not stationed here to be a partizan, but you've stood up to us like a man."

An hour later as I finished my solitary dinner, the electric lights flickered and died, and the engines began their throb. Under cover of the darkness we were slipping out of Gibraltar. I leaned my arms on the table and scanned the remains of my feast by the light of my one sad candle, not thinking of what I saw, or of the various calls for help I had been dispatching, or of the sailor grimly mounting guard outside my door. I was remembering a girl, a girl with ruddy hair and a wild-rose flush and great, gray, starry eyes, a girl that by all the rules of the game I should have handed over to those who represented the countries she was duping, a girl that I had found I had to shield when I came face to face with the issue.

CHAPTER IX

THE BLACK BUTTERFLIES

The Turin-Paris express - the most direct, the Italians call it - was too popular by half to suit the taste of morose beings who wished for solitude. With great trouble and pains I had ferreted out a single vacant compartment; but as four o'clock sounded and the whistle blew for departure, a belated traveler joined me - worse still, an acquaintance who could not be quite ignored.

The unwelcome intruder was Mr. John Van Blarcom, my late fellow-voyager, and he accepted the encounter with a better grace than I.

"Why, hello!" he greeted me cheerfully. "Going through to France? Glad to see you - but you're about the last man that I was looking for. I got the idea somehow you were planning to stop a while in Rome."

I returned his nod with a curtness I was at no pains to dissemble. Then I reproached myself, for it was undeniable that on the *Re d'Italia* he had more than once stood my friend. He had offered me a timely warning, which I had flouted; he had obligingly confirmed my statement in my grueling third degree. Yet despite this, or because of it, I didn't like him; nor did I like his patronizing, complacent manner, which seemed fairly to shriek at me, "I told you so!"

"Changed my plans," I acknowledged with a lack of cordiality that failed to ruffle him. He had hung up his overcoat and installed himself facing me, and was now making preparations for lighting a fat cigar.

"Well," he commented, with a chuckle of raillery, after this operation, "the last time I saw you you were in a pretty tight corner, eh? You can't say it was my fault, either; I'd have put you wise if you'd listened. But you weren't taking any - you knew better than I did - and you strafed me, as the Dutchies say, to the kaiser's taste."

"Good advice seldom gets much thanks, I believe," was my grumpy comment, which he unexpectedly chose to accept as an apology and with a large, fine, generous gesture to blow away.

"That's all right," he declared. "I'm not holding it against you. We've all got to learn. Next time you won't be so easy caught, I guess. It makes a man do some thinking when he gets a dose like you did; and those chaps at Gibraltar certainly gave you a rough deal!"

"On the contrary," I differed shortly, - I wasn't hunting sympathy, - "considering all the circumstances, I think they were extremely fair."

"Not to shoot you on sight? Well, maybe." He was grinning. "But I guess you weren't hunting for a chance to spend two days cooped up in a cabin that measured six feet by five."

"It had advantages. One of them was solitude," I responded dryly. "And it was less unpleasant than being relegated to a six-by-three grave. See here, I don't enjoy this subject! Suppose we drop it. The fact is, I've never understood why you came to my rescue on that occasion, you didn't owe me any civility, you know, and you had to - well - we'll say draw on your imagination when you claimed you saw what I threw overboard that night."

"Sure, I lied like a trooper," he admitted placidly. "Glad to do it. You didn't break any bones when you strafed me, and anyhow, I felt sorry for you. It always goes against me to see a fellow being played!"

Thanks to my determined coolness, the conversation lapsed. I buried myself in the Paris "Herald," but found I could not read. Simmering with wrath, I lived again the ill-starred voyage his words recalled to me, breathed the close smothering air of the cabin that had held me prisoner, tasted the knowledge that I was watched like any thief. An armed sailor had stood outside my door by day and by night; and a dozen times I had longed to fling open that frail partition, seize the man by the collar, and hurl him far away.

Glancing out at the landscape, I saw that Turin lay back of us and that our track was winding through dark chestnut forests toward the heights. Confound Van Blarcom's reminiscences and the thoughts they had set stirring! In ambush behind my paper I gloomily relived the past.

Our ship, following sealed instructions, had changed her course at Gibraltar, conveying us by way of the Spanish coast to Genoa instead of Naples. From my port-hole I had gazed glumly on blue skies and bright, blue waters, purple hills, and white-walled cities, and fishing boats with patched, gaudy sails and dark-complexioned crews. Then Genoa rose from the sea, tier after tier of pink and green and orange houses and shimmering groves of olive trees; and I was summoned to the salon, to face the captain of the port, the chief of the police of the city, and their bedizened suites.

Surrounded by plumes and swords and gold lace, I maintained my innocence and heard Jack Herriott, on his opportune arrival, pour forth in weird, but fluent, Italian an account of me that must have surrounded me in the eyes of all present with a golden halo, and that firmly established me in their minds as the probable next President of the United States. Thanks to these exaggerations and to various confirmatory cable-grams - Dunny had plainly set the wires humming on receiving my S.O.S., - I found myself a free man, at price of putting my signature to a statement of it all. I shook the hand of the ever non-committal Captain Cecchi, and left the ship. And an hour after good old Jack was gazing at me in wrath unconcealed as I informed him that I was in the mood for neither gadding, nor social intercourse, and had made up my mind to proceed immediately to duty at the Front.

"You've been seasick; that's what ails you," he said, diagnosing my condition. "Oh, I don't expect you to admit it - no man ever did that. But you wait and see how you feel when we've had a few meals at the Grand Hotel in Rome!"

This culinary bait leaving me cold, he lost his temper, expressed a hope that the Germans would blow my ambulance to smithereens, and assured me that the next time I brought the Huns' papers across the ocean I might extricate myself without his assistance from what might ensue. However, though he has a bark, Jack possesses no bite worth mentioning. He even saw me off when I left by the north-bound train.

Leaning moodily forward, I looked again from the window and wished I might hurry the creaking, grinding revolution of the wheels. We were climbing higher and higher among the mountains. The chestnuts, growing scanter, were replaced by dark firs and pines. Streams came winding down like icy crystal threads; the little rivers we crossed looked blue and glacial; pale-pink roses and mountain flowers showed themselves as we approached the peaks. A polite official, entering, examined our papers; and with snow surrounding us and cold clear air blowing in at the window, we left Bardonnecchia, the last of the frontier towns.

I was speeding toward France; but where was the girl of the *Re d'Italia*? To what dubious rendezvous, what haunt of spies, had she hurried, once ashore? The thought of her stung my vanity almost beyond endurance. She had pleaded with me that night, swayed against me trustingly, appealed to me as to a chivalrous gentleman and, having competently pulled the wool over my eyes, had laughed at me in her sleeve.

I had held myself a canny fellow, not an easy prey to adventurers; a fairly decent one, too, who didn't lie to a king's officer or help treasonable plots. Yet had I not done just those things by my silence on the steamer? And for what reason? Upon my soul I didn't know, unless because she had gray eyes.

"Hang it all!" I exclaimed, flinging my unlucky paper into a corner, and becoming aware too late that Van Blarcom was observing me with a grin.

"I've got the black butterflies, as the French say," I explained savagely. "This mountain travel is maddening; one might as well be a snail."

"Sure, a slow train's tiresome," agreed Van Blarcom. "Specially if you're not feeling overpleased with life anyway," he added, with a knowing smile.

An angry answer rose to my lips, but the Mont Cenis tunnel opportunely enveloped us, and in the dark half-hour transit that followed I regained my self-control. It was not worth while, I decided, to quarrel with the fellow, to break his head or to give him the chance of breaking mine. After all, I thought low-spiritedly, what right had I to look down on him? We were pot and kettle, indistinguishably black. It was true that he had perjured himself upon the liner; but so, in spirit if not in words, had I!

Thus reflecting, I saw the train emerge from the tunnel, felt it jar to a standstill in the station of Modane, and, in obedience to staccato French outcries on the platform, alighted in the frontier town. Followed by Van Blarcom and preceded by our porters, I strolled in leisurely fashion towards the customs shed. The air was clear, chilly, invigorating; snowy peaks were thick and near. And the scene was picturesque, dotted as it was with mounted bayonets and blue territorial uniforms - reminders that boundary lines were no longer jests and that strangers might not enter France unchallenged in time of war.

Van Blarcom's elbow at this juncture nudged me sharply.

"Say, Mr. Bayne," he was whispering, "look over there, will you? What do you know about that?"

I looked indifferently. Then blank dismay took possession of me. Across the shed, just visible between rows of trunks piled mountain high, stood Miss Esme Falconer, as usual only too well worth seeing from fur hat to modish shoe.

"Ain't that the limit," commented the grinning Van Blarcom; "us three turning up again, all together like this? Well, I guess she won't have to call a policeman to stop you talking to her. You know enough this time to steer pretty clear of her. Isn't that so?"

But I had wheeled upon him; the coincidence was too striking!

"Look here!" I demanded, "are you following that young lady? Is that your business on this side?"

"No!" he denied disgustedly, retreating a step. "Never saw her from the time we docked till this minute; never wanted to see her! Anyhow, what's the glare for? Suppose I was?"

"It's rather strange, you'll admit." I was regarding him fixedly. "You seemed to have a good deal of infor- mation about her on the ship. Yet when that affair occurred at Gibraltar, you were as dumb as an oyster. Why didn't you tell the captain and the English officers the things you knew?"

"Well, I had my reasons," he replied defiantly. "And at that, I don't see as you've got anything on me, Mr. Bayne. You're no fool. You put two and two together quick enough to know darned well who planted those papers in your baggage; so if you thought it needed telling, why didn't you tell it yourself?"

"I don't know who put them there," I denied hastily, "except that he was a pale little runt of a German, pretending to be a thief, who will wish he had died young if I ever see him again."

An inspector had just passed my traps through with bored indifference. I turned a huffy back on Van Blarcom and went to stand in line before a door which harbored, I was told, a special commission for the examination of passports and the admission of travelers into France.

Reaching the inner room in due course, I saluted three uniformed men who sat round an unimposing wooden table, exhibited the *vise* that Jack Herriott had secured for me at Genoa, and was welcomed to the land. Then I stepped forth on the platform, retrieved my porter and my baggage, and placed myself near the door to wait until the girl should come.

I must have been a grim sort of sentinel as I stood there watching. I knew what I had to do, but I detested it with all my heart. There was one thing to be said for this Miss Falconer - she had courage. She was pressing on to French soil without lingering a day in Italy, though she must be aware that by so swift a move she was risking suspicion, discovery, death.

As moment after moment dragged past, I grew uneasy.

Would she come out at all? Could she win past those trained, keen-eyed men? The more I thought of it, the more desperate seemed the game she was playing. This little Alpine town, high among the peaks, surrounded by pines and snow, had been a setting for tragedies since the war began. These territorials with their muskets were not mere supers, either. But no! She was emerging; she was starting toward the *rapide*. There, no doubt, a reserved compartment was awaiting her, and once inside its shelter, she would not appear again.

I drew a deep breath in which resolve and distaste were mingled. She had crossed the frontier, but she was not in Paris yet. I couldn't shirk the thing twice, knowing as I did her charm, her beauty, her air of proud, spirited graciousness - all the tools that equipped her. I couldn't, if I was ever again to hold my head before a Frenchman, let her pass on, so daring and dangerous and resourceful, to do her work in France.

As she approached, I stepped in front of her, lifting my hat.

"This is a great surprise, Miss Falconer," said I.

CHAPTER X

DINNER FOR TWO

I was prepared for fear, for distress, for pleading as I confronted Miss Falconer; the one thing I hadn't expected was that she should seem pleased at the meeting, but she did. She flushed a little, smiled brightly, and held out her gloved hand to me.

"Why, Mr. Bayne! I am so glad!" she exclaimed in frankly cordial tones.

The crass coolness of her tactics, with its implied rating of my intelligence, was the very bracer I needed for a most unpleasant task. I accepted her hand, bowed over it formally, and released it. Then I spoke with the most impersonal courtesy in the world.

"And I," I declared coolly, "am delighted, I assure you. It is great luck meeting you like this; and I will not let you slip away. I suppose that when we board the train they will serve us a meal of some sort. Won't you give me the pleasure of having you for my guest?"

The brightness had left her face as she sensed my attitude. She drew back, regarding me in a rebuffed, bewildered way.

"Thank you, no. I am not hungry."

By Jove, but she was an actress! I should have sworn I had hurt her if I hadn't known the truth.

"Don't say that!" I protested. "Of course it is unconventional to dine with a stranger; but then so is almost everything that is happening to you and me. Think of those lord high executioners in there round the table. See this platform with its guards and bayonets and guns. And then remember our odd experiences on the *Re d'Italia*. Won't you risk one more informality and come and dine?"

She hesitated a moment, watching me steadily; then, with proud reluctance, she walked beside me toward the train.

"You helped me once," she said, her eyes averted now, "and I haven't forgotten. I don't understand at all, - but I shall do as you say."

The passengers were being herded aboard by eager, bustling officials. I saw my baggage and the girl's installed, disposed of the porters, and guided my companion to the *wagon* restaurant. The horn was sounding as we entered, and at six-thirty promptly, just as I put Miss Falconer in her chair, we pulled out of the snowy station of Modane.

As I studied the menu, the girl sat with lowered lashes, all things about her, from her darkened eyes and high head to her pallor, proclaiming her feeling of offense, her sense of hurt. She knew her game, I admitted, and she had first-class weapons. Though she could not weaken my resolution, she made my beginning hard.

"We are going to have a discouraging meal," I gossiped procrastinatingly. "But, since we are in France, it will be a little less horrible than the usual dining-car. The wine is probably hopeless; I suggest Evian or Vichy. These radishes look promising. Will you have some?"

"No. I am not hungry," she repeated briefly. "Won't you please tell me what you have to say?"

Though I didn't in the least want them, I ate a few of the radishes just to show that I was not abashed by her haughty, reproachful air. Other passengers were strolling in. Here was Mr. John Van Blarcom, who, at the sight of Miss Falconer and myself to all appearances cozily established for a tete-a-tete meal, stopped in his tracks and fastened on me the hard, appraising scrutiny that a policeman might turn on a hitherto respectable acquaintance discovered in converse with some notorious crook. For an instant he seemed disposed to buttonhole me and remonstrate. Then he shrugged his stocky shoulders, the gesture indicating that one can't save a fool from his folly, and established himself at a near-by table, from which coign of vantage he kept us under steady watch.

Given such an audience, my outward mien must be impeccable.

"There is something," I admitted cautiously, "that I want to say to you. But I wish you would eat something first. People are watching us," I added beneath my breath as the soup appeared.

She took a sip under protest, and then replaced her spoon and sat with fingers twisting her gloves and eyes fixed smolderingly on mine. I shifted furtively in my seat. This was a charming experience. I was being, from my point of view, almost quixotically generous; yet with one glance she could make me feel like a bully and a brute.

"I am sure," I stumbled, fumbling desperately with my serviette, "that you came over without realizing what war conditions are. Strangers aren't wanted just now. Travel is dangerous for women. You may think me all kinds of a presumptuous idiot, - I shan't blame you, - but I am going to urge you most strongly to go home."

Whatever she had looked for, obviously it was not that.

"Mr. Bayne," she exclaimed, regarding me wonderingly, "what do you mean?"

"Just this, Miss Falconer," I answered with almost Teutonic ruthlessness. Confound it! I couldn't sit here forever bullying her; sheer desperation lent me strength. "The *Espagne* sails from Bordeaux on Saturday, I see by the Herald, and if I were you, I should most certainly be on board. In fact, if you lose the chance, I am sure you'll regret it later. The French police authorities are - er - very inquisitive about foreigners; and if you stop in France in these anxious times, I think it likely that they may - well -"

She drew a quick, hard breath as I trailed off into silence. Her eyes, darkened, horrified, were gazing full into mine.

"You wouldn't tell them about me! You couldn't be so cruel!" The words came almost fiercely, yet with a sound like a stifled sob.

By its sheer preposterousness the speech left me dumb a moment, and then gave me back the self-possession I had been clutching at throughout the meal. For the first time since entering I sat erect and squared my shoulders. I even confronted her with a rather glittering smile.

"I am very sorry," I said, with a cool stare, "if I appear so; but I am consideration itself compared with the people you would meet in Paris, say. That's the very point I'm making - that you can't travel now in comfort. I'm simply trying to spare you future contretemps, Miss Falconer; such as I had on the *Re d'Italia*, you may recall."

She leaned impulsively across the table.

"Oh, Mr. Bayne, I knew it! You are angry about that wretched extra, and you have a right to be. Of course you thought it cowardly of me - yes, and ungrateful - to stand there without a word and let those officers question you. Mr. Bayne, if the worst had come to the worst, I should have spoken, I should, indeed; but I had to wait. I had to give myself every chance. It meant so much, so much! You had nothing to hide from them. You were certain to win through. And then, you seemed so undisturbed, so unruffled, so able to take care of yourself; I knew you were not afraid. It was different with me. If they began to suspect, if they learned who I was, I could never have entered France. This route through Italy was my one hope! I am so sorry. But still -"

Hitherto she had been appealing; but now she defied frankly. That tint of hers, like nothing but a wild rose, drove away her pallor; her gray eyes flamed.

"But still," she flashed at me, "you won't inform on me just for that? I asked you to help me; you were free to refuse - and you agreed! Because it inconvenienced you a little, are you going to turn police agent?" Her red lips twisted proudly, scornfully. "I don't believe it, Mr. Bayne!"

I laughed shortly. She was indeed an artist.

"I wasn't thinking of that particular episode - " I began.

"But you did resent it. I saw it when you first joined me. And I was so glad to see you - to have the chance of thanking you!" she broke in, smoldering still.

"No, I didn't resent it. I didn't even blame you. If I blamed any one, Miss Falconer, it would certainly be myself. I've concluded I ought not to go about without a keeper. My gullibility must have amused you tremendously." I laughed.

"I never thought you gullible," she denied, suddenly wistful. "I thought you very generous and very chivalrous, Mr. Bayne."

This was carrying mockery too far.

"I am afraid," I said meaningly, "that the authorities at Gibraltar would take a less flattering view. For instance, if those Englishmen learned that I had refrained from telling them of our meeting at the St. Ives, I should hear from them, I fancy."

Again her eyes were widening. What attractive eyes she had!

"The St. Ives?" she repeated wonderingly. "Why should that interest them? What do you mean?" Then, suddenly, she bent forward, propped her elbows on the table, and amazed me with a slow, astonished, comprehending smile. "I see!" she murmured, studying me intently. "You thought that I screened the man who hid those papers, that I crossed the ocean on - similar business, perhaps even that on this side I was to take the documents from your trunk?"

"Naturally," I rejoined stiffly. "And I congratulate you. It was a brilliant piece of work; though, as its victim, I fail to see it in the rosiest light."

"I understand," she went on, still smiling faintly. "You thought I was - well - Look over yonder."

Her glance, seeking the opposite wall unostentatiously, directed my attention to a black-lettered, conspicuously posted sign:

BE SILENT!

BE MISTRUSTFUL!

THE EARS OF THE ENEMY ARE LISTENING!

Thus it shouted its warning, like the thousands of its kind that are scattered about the trains, the boats, the railroad stations, and all the public places of France.

"You thought I was the ears of the enemy, didn't you?" the girl was asking. "You thought I was a German agent. I might have guessed! Well, in that case it was kind of you not to hand me over to the Modane gendarmes. I ought to thank you. But I wasn't so suspicious when they searched your trunk and found the papers - I simply felt that they must be crazy to think you could be a spy."

I achieved a shrug of my shoulders, a polite air of incredulity; but, to tell the truth, I was a little less skeptical than I appeared. There was something in her manner that by no means suggested pretense. And she had said a true word about the occurrences on the *Re d'Italia*. If appearances meant facts, I myself had been proved guilty up to the hilt.

"Mr. Bayne," she was saying soberly, "I should like you to believe me - please! I am an American, and I have had cause lately to hate the Germans; all my bonds are with our own country and with France. There is some one very dear to me to whom this war has worked a cruel injustice. I have come to try to help that person; and for certain reasons - I can't explain them - I had to come in secret or not at all. But I have done nothing wrong, nothing dishonorable. And so" - again her eyes challenged me - "I shall not sail from Bordeaux on the *Espagne* on Saturday; and you shall choose for yourself whether you will speak of me to the French police."

It was not much of an argument, regarded dispassionately; yet it shook me. With sudden craftiness I resolved to trap her if I could.

"I ought to tell them on the mere chance that they would send you home," I grumbled irritably. "You have no business here, you know, helping people and being suspected and pursued and outrageously annoyed by fools like me. Yes, and by other fools - and worse," I added with feigned sulphurousness, indicated

Marion Polk Angellotti

Van Blarcom. "Miss Falconer, would you mind glancing at the third man on the right - the dark man who is staring at us - and telling me whether or not you ever saw him before you sailed?"

"I am sure I never did," she declared, knitting puzzled brows; "and yet on the *Re d'Italia* he insisted that we had met. It frightened me a little. I wondered whether or not he suspected something. And every time I see him he watches me in that same way."

I was thawing, despite myself.

"There's one other thing," I ventured, "if you won't think me too impertinent: Did you ever hear of a man named Franz von Blenheim?"

"No," she said blankly; "I never did. Who is he?"

No birds out of that covert! If this was acting it was marvelous; there had not been the slightest flicker of confusion in her face.

"Oh, he isn't anybody of importance - just a man," I evaded. "Look here, Miss Falconer, you'll have to forgive me if you can. You shall stay in Paris, and I'll be as silent as the grave concerning you; but I'd like to do more than that. Won't you let me come and call? Really, you know, I'm not such a duffer as you have cause to think me. After we got acquainted you might be willing to trust me with this business, whatever it is. And then, if it's not too desperate, I have friends who could be of help to you." Such was the sop I threw to conscience, the bargain I struck between sober reason and the instinct that made me trust her against all odds. My theories must have been moonshine. Everything was all right, probably. But for the sake of prudence I ought to keep track of her. Besides, I wanted to.

Gratitude and consternation, a most becoming mixture, were in her eyes. She drew back a little.

"Oh, thank you, but that's impossible," she said uncertainly. "I have friends, too; but they can't help me. Nobody can."

"Well," I admitted sadly, "I know the rudiments of manners. I can recognize a conge, but consider me a persistent boor. Come, Miss Falconer, why mayn't I call? Because we are strangers? If that's it, you can assure yourself at the embassy that I am perfectly respectable; and you see I don't eat with my knife or tuck my napkin under my chin or spill my soup."

Again that warm flush.

"Mr. Bayne!" she exclaimed indignantly. "Did I need an introduction to speak to you on the ship, to ask unreasonable favors of you, to make people think you a spy? If you are going to imagine such absurd things, I shall have to -"

"To consent? I hoped you might see it that way."

"Of course," she pondered aloud, "I may find good news waiting. If I do, it will change everything. I could see you once, at least, and let you know. I really owe you that, I think, when you've been so kind to me."

"Yes," I agreed bitterly, with a pang of conscience, "I've been very kind - particularly to-night!"

"Well, perhaps to-night you were just a little difficult." She was smiling, but I didn't mind; I rather liked her mockery now. "Still, even when you thought the worst of me, Mr. Bayne, you kept my secret. And - do you really wish to come to see me?"

"I most emphatically do."

She drew a card from her beaded bag, rummaged vainly for a pencil, ended by accepting mine, and scribbled a brief address.

"Then," she commanded, handing me the bit of pasteboard, "come to this number at noon to-morrow and ask for me. And now, since I'm not to go to prison, Mr. Bayne, I believe I am hungry. This is war bread, I suppose; but it tastes delicious. And isn't the saltless butter nice?"

"And here are the chicken and the salad arriving!" I exclaimed hopefully. "And there never was a French cook yet, however unspeakable otherwise, who failed at those."

What had come to pass I could not have told; but we were eating celestial viands, and my black butterflies having fled away, a swarm of their gorgeous-tinted kindred were fluttering radiantly over Miss Esme Falconer's plate and mine.

CHAPTER XI

IN THE RUE ST.-DOMINIQUE

Arriving in Paris at the highly inconvenient hour of 8 A.M., our *rapide* deposited its breakfastless and grumpy passengers on the platform of the Gare de Lyon, washed its hands of us with the final formality of collecting our tickets, and turned us forth into a gray, foggy morning to seek the food and shelter adapted to our purses and tastes. Every one, of course, emerged from seclusion only at the ultimate moment; and, far from holding any lengthy conversation with Miss Falconer, I was lucky to stumble upon her in the vestibule, help her descend, find a taxi for her at the exit, and see her smile back at me where I stood hatless as she drove away.

While I waited for my own cab I found myself beside Mr. John Van Blarcom, who eyed me with mingled hostility and pity, as if I were a cross between a lunatic and a thief. I returned his stare coolly; indeed, I found it braced me. Left to myself, I had experienced a creeping doubt as to the girl's activities and my own intelligence; but as soon as this fellow glared at me, all my confidence returned.

"Well, Mr. Bayne," he remarked sardonically, breaking the silence, "I suppose you're worrying for fear I'll give you another piece of good advice. Don't you fret! From now on you can hang yourself any way you want to. I'd as soon talk to a man in a padded cell and a strait-jacket. Only don't blame me when the gendarmes come for you next week."

"Oh, go to the devil!" I retorted curtly. It was a relief; I had been wanting to say it ever since we had first met. His jaw shot out menacingly, and for an instant he squared off from me with the look of the professional boxer; but, rather to my disappointment, he thought better of it and turned a contemptuous back.

Upon leaving Genoa I had reserved a room at the Ritz by telegraph. I drove there now, and refreshed myself with a bath and breakfast, casting about me meanwhile for some mode of occupying the hours till noon. There were various tasks, I knew, that should have claimed me; a visit to the police to secure a *carte de sejour*, the presentation of my credentials as an ambulance-driver, a polite notification to friends that I had arrived. These things should have been my duty and pleasure, but somehow they were uninviting. Nothing appealed to me, I realized with sudden enlightenment, except a certain appointment that I had already made.

I went out, to find that the fog was lifting and spring was in the air. Since my dinner the previous night I had felt an odd exhilaration, a pleasure quickened by the staccato sparkle of the French tongue against my ears, the pale-blue uniforms, and gay French faces glimpsed as the train had stopped at various lighted stations. Saluting Napoleon's statue, I strolled up the rue de la Paix, took a table on a cafe pavement, and, ordering a glass of something fizzy for the form of it, sat content and happy, watching the whole gigantic pageant of

Paris in war-time defile before my eyes.

The Cook's tourists and their like, bane of the past, had disappeared; but all nationalities that the world holds seemed to be about. At the next table two Russian officers, with high cheek-bones and wide-set eyes, were drinking, chatting together in their purring, unintelligible tongue. Beyond them a party of Englishmen in khaki, cool-mannered, clear of gaze, were talking in low tones of the spring offensive. The uniforms of France swarmed round me in all their variety, and close at hand a general, gorgeous in red and blue and gold, sat with his hand resting affectionately on the knee of a lad in the horizon blue of a simple poilu, who was so like him that I guessed them at a glance for father and son.

A cab drew up before me, and a Belgian officer with crutches was helped out by the cafe starter, who himself limped slightly and wore two medals on his breast. First one troop and then another defiled across the Place l'Opera: a company of infantry with bayonets mounted, a picturesque regiment of Moroccans, turbaned, of magnificently impassive bearing, sitting their horses like images of bronze. Men of the Flying Corps, in dark blue with wings on their sleeves, strolled past me; and once, roused by exclamations and pointing fingers, I looked up to see a monoplane, light and graceful as a darting bird, skimming above our heads.

Even the faces had a different look, the voices a different ring. It was another country from that of the days of peace. Superb and dauntless, tried by the most searing of fires and not found wanting, France was standing girt with her shining armor , barring the invader from her cities, her villages, her homes.

Deep in my heart - too deep to be talked of often - there had lain always a tenderness for this heroic France. "A man's other country," some wise person had christened it; and so it was for me, since by a chance I had been born here, and since here my father and then my mother had died. I was glad I had run the gauntlet and had reached Paris to do my part in a mighty work. An ambulance drove heavily past me, and with a thrill I wondered how soon I should bend over such a steering wheel, within sound of the great guns.

Leaving the cafe at last, I beckoned a taxi and settled myself on its cushions for a drive. Each new vista that greeted me was enchanting. The pavements, the river, the buildings, the stately bridges, - all held the same soft, silvery tint of pale French gray. In the Place de la Concorde the fountains played as always, but - heart-warming change - the Strasburg statue, symbol of the lost Lorraine and Alsace, no longer drooped under wreaths of mourning, but sat crowned and garlanded with triumphant flowers.

Like diminishing flies, the same eternal swarm of cabs and motors filled the long vista of the Champs-Elysees between the green branches of the chestnut trees. At the end loomed the Arc de Triomphe, beneath which the hordes of the kaiser, in their first madness of conquest, had sworn to march. Farther on, in the Bois, along the shady paths and about the lakes, the French still walked in safety, because on the frontier their soldiers had cried to the Teutons the famous watchword, "You do not pass!" Noon was approaching, and at the Porte Maillot I consulted Miss

Falconer's card.

"Number 630, rue St.-Dominique," I bade the driver, the address falling comfortably on my ears. I knew the neighborhood. Deep in the Faubourg St.-Germain, it was a stronghold of the old noblesse, suggesting eminent respectability, ancient and honorable customs, and family connections of a highly desirable kind. It would be a point in Miss Falconer's favor if I found her conventionally established - a decided point. Along most lines I was in the dark concerning her, but to one dictum I dared to hold: no girl of twenty-two or thereabouts, more than ordinarily attractive, ought to be traveling unchaperoned about this wicked world.

I felt very cheerful, very contented, as my taxi bore me into old Paris. The ancient streets, had a decided lure and charm. Now we passed a quaint church, now a dim and winding alley, now a house with mansard windows or a portal of carved stone. On all sides were buildings that in the old days had been the *hotels* of famous gentry, this one sheltering a Montmorency, that one a Clisson or Soubise. It was just the setting for a romance by Dumas. And, with a chuckle, I felt myself in sudden sympathy with that writer's heroes, none of whom had, it seemed to me, been enmeshed in a mystery more baffling or involved than mine.

"They've got nothing on my affair," I decided, "with their masks and poisoned drinks and swords. For a fellow who leads a cut-and-dried existence generally, I've been having quite a lively time. And now, to cap the climax, I'm going to call on a girl about whom I know just one thing - her name. By Jove, it's exactly like a story! I've got the data. If I had any gray matter I could probably work out the facts.

"Take the St. Ives business. It's plain enough that some one wished those papers on me, intending to unwish them in short order once we got across. The logical suspect, judging by appearances, was Miss Falconer. The little German went out through her room; she was the one person I saw both at the hotel and on the *Re d'Italia*; and she acted in a suspicious manner that first night aboard the ship. But she says she didn't do it, and probably she didn't; it seemed infernally odd, all along, for her to be a spy.

"Still, if she is innocent, who can be responsible? And if that affair didn't bring her over here, what the dickens did? Something mysterious, something dangerous, something that the French police wouldn't appreciate, but that her conscience sanctions - that is all she deigns to say. And why on earth did she ask me to destroy that extra? I thought it was because she was Franz von Blenheim's agent and the paper had an account of him that might have served as a clue to her. She says, though, that she never heard of him. And I may be all kinds of a fool, but it sounded straight.

"Then, there's Van Blarcom, hang him! He seemed to take a fancy to me. He warned me about the girl, but he kept a still tongue to Captain Cecchi and the rest. He lied deliberately, for no earthly reason, to shield me in that interrogation; yet when those papers materialized in my trunk, though he must have thought just what I thought as to Miss Falconer's share in it, he didn't breathe a word. He claimed that he had met her. She said she had never seen him. And then - rather strong for a coincidence - we all three met again on the express. What is he doing on this side? Shadowing her? Nonsense? And yet he seemed almighty keen about her - Oh, hang it! I'm no Sherlock Holmes!"

The taxi pausing at this juncture, I willingly abandoned my attempt at sleuthing and got out in the highest spirits compatible with a strictly correct mien. I dismissed my driver. If asked to remain to *dejeuner*, I should certainly do so. Then, with feelings of natural interest, I gazed at the house before which I stood.

In the outward seeming, at least, it was all that the most fastidious could have required; a gem of Renaissance architecture in its turrets, its quaint, scrolled windows, and the carving of its stone facade. Age and romance breathed from every inch of it. For not less than four hundred years it had watched the changing life of Paris; and even to a lay person like myself a glance proclaimed it one of those ancestral *hotels*, the pride of noble French families, about which many romantic stories cling.

At another time it would have charmed me hugely, but to-day, as I stood gazing, somehow, my spirits fell. Was it the almost sepulchral silence of the place, the careful drawing of every shutter, the fact that the grilled gateway leading to the court of honor was locked? I did not know; I don't know yet; but I had an odd, eerie feeling. It seemed like a place of waiting, of watching, and of gloom.

This was unreasonable; it was even down-right ridiculous. I began to think that late events were throwing me off my base. "It's a house like any other, and a jolly fine old one!" I assured myself, approaching the grilled entrance and producing one of my cards.

An entirely modern electric button was installed there, beneath a now merely ornamental knocker in grotesque

Marion Polk Angellotti

gargoyle form. I pressed it, peering through the iron latticework at the stately court. The answer was prompt. Down the steps of the hotel came a white-headed majordomo, gorgeously arrayed, and so pictorial that he might have been a family retainer stepping from the pages of an old tale.

There was something queer about him, I thought, as he crossed the courtyard; just as there was about the house, I appended doggedly, with growing belief. His air was tremulous, his step slow, his gaze far-off and anxious.

"For Miss Falconer, who waits for me," I announced in French, offering him my card through the grille.

He bowed to me with the deference of a Latin, the grand manner of an ambassador; but he made no motion to let me in.

"Mademoiselle," he replied, "sends all her excuses, all her regrets to monsieur, but she leaves Paris within the hour and, therefore may not receive."

I had feared it for a good sixty seconds. None the less, it was a blow to me. My suspicions, never more than half laid, promptly raised their heads again.

"Have the kindness," I requested, with a calm air of command that I had known to prove hypnotic, "to convey my card to mademoiselle, and to say that I beg of her, before her departure, one little instant of speech."

But the old fellow's faded blue eyes were gazing past me, hopelessly sad, supremely mournful. What the deuce ailed him? I wondered angrily. The thing was almost weird. Of a sudden, with irritation, yet with dread, too, I felt myself on the threshold of a house of tragedy. The man might, from the look of him, have been watching some loved young master's bier.

"Mademoiselle regrets greatly," he intoned, "but she may not receive. Mademoiselle sends this letter to monsieur that he may understand." He passed me, through the locked grille, a slender missive; then he saluted me once more and, still staring before him with that fixed, uncanny look, withdrew.

CHAPTER XII

THE GRAY CAR

I was divided between exasperation and pity. The old fellow was in a bad way; I felt sorry for him. Dunny had an ancient butler, a household institution, who had presided over our destinies since my childhood and would, I fancied, look something like this if he should hear that I was dead. But in heaven's name, what was wrong here, and was nothing in the world clear and aboveboard any longer? On the chance that the letter might enlighten me I tore open the envelope and read with mixed feelings the following note:

DEAR Mr. BAYNE:

The news that I found waiting for me was not good, as I had hoped. It was bad, very bad - as bad as news can be. I must leave Paris at once, and I can see no one, talk to no one, before I go. Please believe that I am sorry, and that I shall never forget the kindness you showed me on the ship.

Sincerely yours,

ESME FALCONER.

That was all. Well, the episode was ended - ended,

moreover, with a good deal of cavalierness. She had treated me like a meddlesome, pertinacious idiot who had insisted on calling and had to be taught his place. This was a Christian country where the formalities of life prevailed; I could not - unless escorted and countenanced by gendarmes - seize upon a club and batter down that grille.

I was resentful, wrathful, in the very deuce of a humor. Black gloom settled over me. I admitted that Van Blarcom had been right. I recalled the girl's vague explanations as we sat over our dinner; her denials, unbolstered save by my willingness to accept them; all the chain of incriminating circumstances that I had pondered over in the cab. Her charm and the mystery that enveloped her had thrilled and stirred me; she had seen it. To gain a few hours' leeway she had once again duped me; and this hotel, with its deceptive air of family and respectability, was a blind, a rendezvous, another such setting for intrigue as the St. Ives.

Her work might be already accomplished. Perhaps she had left Paris. I told myself with some savageness that I did not know and did not care. From the first my presence in this luridly adventurous galley had been incongruous; I would get back with all despatch to the Ritz and the orderly world it typified.

I had gone perhaps twenty feet when a grating noise attracted me. Glancing back across my shoulder, I saw that the old majordomo was unlocking and setting wide the gate. The hum of a self-starter reached me faintly, and a moment later there rolled slowly forth a dark-blue touring-car of luxurious aspect, driven by a chauffeur whose coat and cap and goggles gave him rather the appearance of a leather brownie, and bearing in the tonneau Miss Falconer, elaborately coated and veiled.

She was turning to the right, not the left; she would not pass me. I stood transfixed, watching from my post against the wall. As the car crept by the old major-domo, he saluted, and she spoke to him, bending forward for a moment to rest her fingers on his sleeve.

"Be of courage, Marcel, my friend! All will be well if *le bon Dieu* wills it," I heard her say. Then to the chauffeur she added: "*En avant, Georges! Vite, a* Bleau!" The motor snorted as the car gained speed, and they were gone.

The ancient Marcel, reentering, locked the grille behind him. I was left alone, more astounded than before. The girl's kind speech to the old servant, her gentle tones, her womanly gesture, had been bewilde-ring. Despite all the accusing features her case offered, I should have said just then, as I watched Miss Esme Falconer, that she was nothing more or less than a superlatively nice girl.

"Honk! Honk! Honk!"

I swung round, startled. A moment earlier the length and breadth of the street had stretched before me, empty; yet now I saw, sprung apparently out of nowhere, a long, lean, gray car, low-built like a racer, carrying four masked and goggled men. Steadily gaining speed as it came, it bore down upon me and, after grazing me with its running-board and nearly deafening me with the powerful blast of its horn, flew on down the street and vanished in Miss Falconer's wake.

Trying to clarify my emotions, I stared after this Juggernaut. Was it merely the sudden appearance of the thing, its look, so lean and snake-like and somber-colored, and the muffled air of its occupants that had struck me as sinister when it went flashing by? I wasn't sure, but I had formed the impression that these men were following Miss Falconer. A patently foolish idea! And yet, and yet -

My experiences at the St. Ives and on the *Re d'Italia* had contributed to my education. I could no longer deny that melodrama, however unwelcome, did sometimes intrude itself into the most unlikely lives. The girl was bound somewhere on a secret purpose. Could these four men be her accomplices? Were they going too?

"*A* Bleau!"

Those had been her words to the chauffeur; for Bleau, then, she was bound. But where did such a place exist? I had never heard of it; and yet I possessed, I flattered myself, through the medium of motor-touring, a fairly comprehensive knowledge of the map of France.

The affair was becoming a veritable nightmare. It seemed incredible that a few minutes earlier I had resolved to wash my hands of it all. If the girl had a disloyal mission, it was my plain duty to intercept her. I could not denounce her to the police. I didn't analyze the why and wherefore of my inability to take this step; I simply knew and accepted it. If I interfered with what she was doing, I must interfere quietly, alone.

Ordinarily I have as much imagination as a turnip, but now I indulged in a sudden and surprising flight of fancy. Might it be, I found myself wondering, that the men in the gray care were not Miss Falconer's accomplices, but her pursuers? In that case, high as was her courage, keen as were her wits, - I found myself thinking of them with a sort of pride, - she was laboring under a handicap of which she could not dream.

Again, where had that long, lean, pursuing streak sprung from? Could it have lurked somewhere in the neighborhood, spying on the hotel that Miss Falconer had just left, waiting for her to emerge? I was aware of my absurdity, but I couldn't put an end to it; with each instant that went by my uneasiness seemed to grow. So I yielded, not without qualms as to whether the quarter would take me for a gibbering idiot. Grimly and doggedly I stalked the length of the rue St.-Dominique, and the stately houses on both sides seemed to scorn me, their shutters to eye me pityingly, as I peered to right and left for the possible cache of the car.

And within four hundred feet I found it. Against all reason and probability, there it was. At my left there opened unostentatiously one of those short, dark, neglected blind alleys so common in the older part of Paris, with the houses meeting over it and forming an arched roof. Running back twenty feet or so, it ended in a blank wall of stone; and, amid the dust and debris that covered its rough paving, I distinctly made out the tracks of tires, with between them, freshly spilt, a tiny, gleaming pool of oil.

At this psychological moment a taxicab came meandering up the street. It was unoccupied, but its red flag was turned down. The driver shook his head vigorously as I signaled him.

"I go to my *dejeuner*, Monsieur!" he explained.

"On the contrary," said I fiercely, "you go to the tourist bureau of Monsieur Cook in the Place de l'Opera, at the greatest speed the *sergents de ville* allow!"

I must have mesmerized him, for he took me there obediently, casting hunted glances back at me from time to time when the traffic momentarily halted us, as if fearing to find that I was leveling a pistol at his head.

It being noon, the office of the tourist bureau was almost deserted, a single, bored-looking, young French clerk keeping vigil behind the travelers' counter. With the sociable instinct of his nation he brightened up at my appearance.

"I want," I announced, "to ask about trains to Bleau."

For a moment he looked blank; then he smiled in understanding.

"Monsieur is without doubt an artist," he declared.

I was not, decidedly; but the words had been an affirmation and not a question. It seemed clear that for some cryptic reason I ought to have been an artist. Accordingly, I thought it best to bow.

He seemed childishly pleased with his acumen.

"Monsieur will understand," he explained, "that before the war we sold tickets to many artists, who, like monsieur, desired to paint the old mill on the stream near Bleau. It has appeared at the Salon many times, that mill! Also, we have furnished tickets to archaeologists who desired to see the ruins of the antique chapel, a veritable gem! But monsieur has not an archaeologist's aspect. Therefore, monsieur is an artist."

"Perfectly," I agreed.

"As to the trains," he continued contentedly, "there is but one a day. It departs at two and a half hours, upon the Le Moreau route. Monsieur will be wise to secure, before leaving Paris, a safe-conduct from the *prefecture*; for the village is, as one might say, on the edge of the zone of war. With such a permit monsieur will find his visit charming; regrettable incidents will not occur; undesirable conjectures about monsieur's identity will not be roused. I should strongly advise that monsieur provide himself with such a credential, though it is not, perhaps, absolutely *de rigueur*."

Back in my room at the Ritz, I consulted my watch. It was a quarter of two; certainly time had marched apace. Should I, like a sensible man, descend to the restaurant and enjoy a sample of the justly famous cuisine of the hotel? Or should I throw all reason overboard and post off on - what was it Dunny had called my mission - a wild-goose chase?

I glanced at myself in the mirror and shook a disapproving head. "You're no knight-errant," I told my impassive image. "You're too correct, too indifferent-looking altogether. Better not get beyond your depth!" I decided for luncheon, followed by a leisurely knotting of the threads of my Parisian acquaintance. Then, as if some malign hypnotist had projected it before me, I saw again a vision of that flashing, lean, gray car.

"I'm hanged if I don't have a shot at this thing!"

The words seemed to pop out of my mouth entirely of their own accord. By no conscious agency of my own, I found myself madly hurling collars, handkerchiefs, toilet articles, whatever I seemed likeliest to need in a brief journey, into a bag. Lastly I realized that I was standing, hat in hand, overcoat across my arm, considering my revolver, and wondering whether taking it with me would be too stagy and absurd.

"No more so than all the rest of it," I decided, shrugging. Dropping the thing into my pocket, I made for the *ascenseur*.

"I shan't be back to-night," I informed the hall porter woodenly. "Or perhaps to-morrow night. But, of course, I'm keeping my room."

With his wish for a charming trip to speed me, I left the Ritz, and luckily no vision was vouchsafed me of the condition in which I should return: Two crutches, a bandaged head, an utterly disreputable aspect; my bedraggled state equaled - and this I would maintain with swords and pistols if necessary - that of any poilu of them all.

As I drove toward the station, various headlines stared at me from the kiosks. "Franz von Blenheim Rumored on Way to France," ran one of them. Hang Franz. I had had enough of him to last the rest of my life. "Duke of Raincy-la-Tour Still Missing," proclaimed another. I knew something about him, too; but what? Ah, to be sure, he was the Firefly of France, the hero of the Flying Corps, the young nobleman of whose suspected treason I had read in that extra on the ship. In that

damned extra, I amended, with natural feeling. For it
was like Rome; everything seemed to lead its way.

CHAPTER XIII

AT THE THREE KINGS

"What's the best hotel in the place?" I inquired somewhat dubiously. The man in the blouse, who had performed the three functions of opening my compartment-door, carrying my bag to the gate, and relieving me of my ticket, achieved a thoroughly Gallic shrug.

"Monsieur," said he, "what shall I tell you? The best hotel, the worst hotel - these are one. There is only the Hotel des Trois Rois in the town of Bleau. Let monsieur proceed by the street of the Three Kings and he will reach it. Formerly there was an omnibus, but now the horses are taken. And if they remained, who could drive them with all the men at the war?"

Carrying my bag and feeling none too amiable, I set off along the indicated route. In Paris, rushing from the rue St.-Dominique to Cook's office, from that office to the hotel, from the hotel to the *gare*, I had been a sort of whirling dervish with no time for sober thought. My trip of four hours on a slow, stuffy, crowded train had, however, afforded me ample leisure; and I had spent the time in grimly envisaging the possibilities that, I decided, were most likely to befall.

First and foremost disagreeable; that the men in the

Marion Polk Angellotti

gray automobile were helping Miss Falconer in some nefarious business. In this case, it would be up to me to fight the gentlemen single-handed, rescue the girl, and escort her back to Paris, all without scandal. Easier said than done!

Second possibility: that Miss falconer, pausing at Bleau only en route, might already have departed, and that I would be left with my journey for my pains.

Third: that the gray car had no connection with her; that she had some entirely blameless errand. I hoped so, I was sure. If this proved true, I was bound to stand branded as a meddling, officious idiot, one who, in defiance of the most elementary social rules, persisted in trailing her against her will. Vastly pleasant, indeed!

Fuming, I shifted my bag from one hand to the other and walked faster. Night was falling, but it was not yet really dark, and I formed a clear enough notion of the village as I traversed it. It was one of the hundreds of its kind which make an artists' paradise of France. Entirely unmodernized, it was the more picturesque for that. If I tripped sometimes on the roughly paved street I could console myself with the knowledge that these cobbles, like the odd, jutting houses rising on both sides of them, were at least three hundred years old. Green woods, clear against a background of rosy sunset, ran up to the very borders of the town. I passed a little, gray old church. I crossed a quaint bridge built over a winding stream lined with dwellings and broken by mossy washing-stones. It was all very peaceful, very simple, and very rustic. Without second sight I could not possibly have visioned the grim little drama for which it was to serve as setting.

A blue sign with gilded letters beckoned me, and I paused to read it. The Touring Club of France recommended to the passing stranger the Hotel of the Three Kings. Here I was, then. From the street a dark, arched, stone passage of distinctly *moyen-age* flavor led me into a courtyard paved with great square cobbles, round the four sides of which were built the walls of the inn. Winding, somewhat crazy-looking, stone staircases ran up to the galleries from which the bedroom doors informally opened; vines, as yet leafless, wreathed the gray walls and framed the shuttered windows; before me I glimpsed a kitchen with a magnificent oaken ceiling and a medieval fireplace in which a fire roared redly; and at my right yawned what had doubtless been a stable once upon a time, but with the advent of the motor, had become a primitive garage.

I took the liberty of peering inside. Eureka! There, resting comfortably from its day's labors, stood a dark-blue automobile. If this was not the motor that had brought Miss Falconer from the rue St.-Dominique, it was its twin.

"You'll notice it's alone, though," I told myself. "Where's the gray car?"

My mood was grumpy in the extreme. The inn was charming, but I knew from sad experience that no place combines all attractions, and that a spot so picturesque as this would probably lack running water and electric light.

"Bonsoir, Monsieur!"

A buxom, smiling, bare-armed woman had emerged

from the kitchen door. She was plainly the hostess. I set down my bag and removed my hat.

"Madame," I responded, "I wish you a good evening. I desire a room for the night in the Hotel of the Three Kings."

"To accommodate monsieur," she assured me warmly, "will be a pleasure. Monsieur is an artist without doubt?"

I wanted to say "*Et tu, Brute!*" but I didn't. When one came to think of it, I had no very good reason to advance for having appeared at Bleau. It wasn't the sort of place into which one would drop from the skies by pure chance, either. I was lucky to find a ready-made explanation.

"But assuredly," said I.

She disappeared into the kitchen, returned immediately with a candle, and led me up the stone staircase on the left of the courtyard, talking volubly all the while.

"We have had many artists here," she declared; "many friends of monsieur, doubtless. Since monsieur is of that fine profession, his room will be but four francs daily; his dinner, three francs; his little breakfast, a franc alone."

"Madame," I responded, "it is plain that the high cost of living, which terrorizes my country, does not exist at Bleau."

Equally plain, I thought pessimistically, was the explanation. My saddest forebodings were realized; if the name of the hotel meant anything and three kings ever tarried here, that conjunction of sovereigns had put up with housing of a distinctly primitive sort. My room was clean, I acknowledged thankfully, but that was all I could say for it. I eyed the bowl and pitcher gloomily, the hard-looking bed, the tiny square of carpeting in the center of the stone floor.

"Your house, Madame," I suggested craftily, with a view to reconnoissance, "is, of course, full?"

She heaved a sigh.

"It is war-time, Monsieur," she lamented. "None travel now. Yet why should I mourn, since I make enough to keep me till the war is ended and my man comes home? There are those who eat here daily at the noon hour - the cure, the mayor, the mayor's secretary, sometimes the notary of the town, as well. And to-night I have two guests, monsieur and the young lady - the nurse who goes to the hospital at Carrefonds with the great new remedy for burns and scars. *Au revoir, Monsieur*. In one little moment I will send the hot water, and in half an hour monsieur shall dine."

I closed the door behind her and flung down my bag, fuming. So Miss Falconer was a nurse, carrying a panacea to the wounded, doubtless a specimen of the sensational new remedy just recognized by the medical authorities, of which the one newspaper I had glanced through in Paris had been full. The masquerade was too preposterous to gain an instant's credence. It gave me, as the French say, furiously to think; it resolved all doubts.

I felt inexplicably angry, then preternaturally cool and

competent. For the first time since the Modane episode I was my clear-sighted self. I had been trying futilely to blindfold my eyes, to explain the inexplicable, to be unaware of the obvious. Now with a sort of grim relief I looked the facts in the face.

My hot water appearing, I made a sketchy toilet, and then descended to the courtyard where I lounged and smoked. My state of mind was peculiar. As I struck a match I noticed with a queer pride that my hand was steady. With a cold, almost sardonic clarity, I thought of Miss Falconer. First a prosperous tourist, next a dweller in an aristocratic French mansion, then a nurse. She equaled, I told myself, certain heroines of our Sunday supplements, queens of the smugglers, moving spirits of the diamond ring.

Upstairs in the right-hand gallery a door opened. A light footstep sounded on the winding stairs. The critical moment was upon me; she was coming. I threw away my cigarette and advanced.

She was playing her part, I saw, with due regard for detail. Now that her furs were off she stood forth in the white costume, the flowing head-dress, the red cross - all the panoply of the *infirmiere*. She came half-way down the stairs before perceiving me; then, with a low exclamation, grasping the balustrade, she stood still.

I didn't even pretend surprise. What was the use of it?

"Good-evening, Miss Falconer," was all I said.

It seemed a long time before she answered. Rigid, uncompromising, she faced me; and I read storm signals in the deep flush of her cheeks, the gray flash of her eyes, the stiffness of her white-draped head.

"Oh, Lord!" I groaned to myself in cold compassion, "she means to bluff it! Can't she see that the game's played out?"

"This is very strange, Mr. Bayne," she was saying idly. "I understood that you were to drive an ambulance at the Front."

How young, how lovely, how glowing she looked as she stood there in her snowy dress. I found myself wondering impersonally what had led her to these devious paths.

"So I am," I responded with accentuated coolness. "My time is valuable; it was a sacrifice to come to Bleau; but I had no choice. What's wrong, Miss Falconer? You don't object to my presence surely? If you go on freezing me like this, I shall think there's something about my turning up here that worries you - upon my soul I shall!"

She should by rights have been trembling, but her eyes blazed at me disdainfully. I felt almost like a caitiff, whatever that may be.

"It doesn't worry me," she denied, with the same crisp iciness, "but it does surprise me. Will you tell me, please, what you are doing here?"

Should I return, "And you?" in a voice of obvious meaning? Should I take a leaf from the book of my hostess and say: "I'm a bit of an artist. I've sketched all over Europe, and I've come to have a go at the old mill that so many fellows try"? Such a claim would just match the assumption of her costume. But no.

"The fact is," I said serenely, "I came straight from the rue St.- Dominique to keep the appointment you forgot."

The announcement, it was plain, exasperated her, for slightly, but undeniably, she stamped one arched, slender, attractively shod foot.

"Mr. Bayne," she demanded, "are you a secret-service agent?"

"Good heavens!" I exclaimed, startled. No!"

"Then I'm sorry. That would have been a better reason for following me than - than the only one there is," she swept on stormily. "You knew I didn't wish to see any one at present. I said so in the note I left. Yet you spied on me and you tracked me deliberately, when I had trusted you with my address. It's outrageous of you. You ought to be ashamed of doing it, Mr. Bayne."

A stunned realization burst on me of the line that she was taking, the position into which, willy-nilly, she was crowding me. I had trailed her here, she assumed, to thrust my company on her; and, upon the surface, I had to own that my behavior really had that air. If I had followed her with equal brazenness along Fifth Avenue, I should have had a chance to explain my conduct to the first police officer who noticed it, later to an indignant magistrate. But, heavens and earth! She knew why I had come. And knowing, how did she dare defy me? I retained just sufficient presence of mind to stare back impassively and to mumble with feeble sarcasm:

"I'm very sorry you think so."

She came down a step.

"Are you?" she asked imperiously. "Then - will you prove it? Will you go back to Paris by to-night's train?"

I had recovered myself.

"There isn't any train to-night," I protested, civil, but adamant. "And - I'm sorry, but if there was I wouldn't take it - not until I've accomplished what I came to do!"

The girl seemed to concentrate all the world's disdain in the look that measured me, running from my head to my unoffending feet, from my feet back to my head.

"Most men would go, Mr. Bayne," she flung at me, her red lips scornful. "But then, most men wouldn't have come, of course. And all you will accomplish is to make me dine up here in this - this wretched, stuffy room." Before I could lift a hand in protest, she had turned, mounted the stairs again, and vanished. The door - shall I own it? - slammed.

CHAPTER XIV

THE PLOT THICKENS

Presently, summoned by the hostess, I went to my lonely meal in a mood that nobody on earth had cause to envy me. One thing was certain: Should it ever be disclosed that Miss Esme Falconer was not a spy, I should lack courage to go on living. Remembering the coolly brazen line I had taken and the assumptions she had drawn from it, I could think of no desert wide enough to hide my confusion, no pit sufficiently deep to shelter my utterly crestfallen head.

In any case, I had not managed my attack at all triumphantly. From the first skirmish the adversary had retired with all the honors on her side. Carrying the matter with a high hand, she had dazed me into brief inaction, and then, as I gave signs of rally, had retreated in what to say the least was a highly strategic way. Well, let her go for the moment! She could scarcely escape me. I would see the thing through, I told myself with growing stubbornness; but I didn't feel that the doing of a civic duty was what it is cracked up to be. Not at all!

I felt the need of a cocktail with a kick to it. But I did not get one. However, the cabbage soup was eatable, if primitive; and, in fact, no part of the dinner could be called distinctly bad.

Having finished my coffee, I went outside feeling more cheerful. It was dark now. A lantern swinging from the entrance cast flickering darts of light about the courtyard, the rough paving-stones, the odd old galleries and stairs. Upstairs a candle shone through the window of Miss Falconer's room. In the kitchen by the great chimney place I could see a leather-clad chauffeur eating, the same fellow that had driven the blue car from the rue St.-Dominique; and while I watched, madame emerged, bearing the girl's dinner tray, which with much groaning and panting she carried up the winding stairs.

It was foolish of Miss Falconer, I thought, to insist on this comedy. She might better have dined with me, heard what I had to say, and yielded with a good grace. However, let her have her dinner in peace and solitude, I resolved magnanimously. The moon had come out, the stars too; I would take a stroll and mature my plans.

Lighting a cigarette, I lounged into the street and addressed myself forthwith to an unhurried tour of Bleau. I was gone perhaps an hour, not a very lengthy interval, but one in which a variety of things can occur, as I was to learn. My walk led me outside the village, down a water path between trees, and even to the famous mill, which was charming. Had I been of the fraternity of artists, as I had claimed, I should have asked no better fate than to come there with canvas and brushes and immortalize the quiet beauty of the scene.

A rustic bridge invited me, and I stood and smoked upon it, listening to the ripple of the half-golden, half-shadowy water, watching the revolutions of the green old wheel. I had laid out my plan of action. On my return to the inn I would insist on an interview with Miss Falconer, and would tell her that either she must return with me to Paris or that the police of Bleau - I supposed it had police - must take a hand.

My metamorphosis into a hero of adventure, racing about the country, visiting places I had never heard of, coolly assuming the control of international spy plots, brutally determining to kidnap women if necessary, was astounding to say the least. That dinner in the St. Ives restaurant rose before me, and I heard again Dunny's charge that I was growing stodgy with advancing years. Suppose he should see me now, involved in these insane developments? He might call me various unflattering things, but not stodgy - not with truth. I chuckled half-heartedly, my last chuckle, by the by, for a long time. Unknown to me and unsuspected, the darker, more deadly side of the adventure was steadily drawing near.

When I entered the courtyard of the Three Kings, the door of the garage stood open, and the first object my eyes met within it was the pursuing gray car. I stared at the thing, transfixed. In the march of events I had forgotten it. I was still gaping at it when madame came hurrying forth.

"I have been watching," she informed me, "for monsieur's return. Friends of his arrived here soon after he left the house."

"The deuce they did!" I thought, dumb-founded. I judged prudence advisable.

"They have names, these friends?" I inquired warily.

"Without doubt, Monsieur," she agreed, "but they did not offer them; and who am I to ask questions of the officers of France? They are bound on a mission, plainly. In time of war those so engaged talk little. They have eaten, and they have gone to their rooms, off the gallery to the west. And the fourth of their party - he alone wears no uniform; he is doubtless of monsieur's land - asked of me a description of my guests, and exclaimed in great delight, saying that monsieur was his old friend, whom he had hoped to find here and with whom he must have speech the very moment that monsieur should return. I know no more."

It was enough.

"He's mistaken," I said shortly. For the moment I really thought that this must be the case.

Her broad, good-natured face was all astonishment.

"But, Monsieur," she burst forth, "he even told me, this gentleman, that such might be monsieur's reply! And in that event he commanded me to beg monsieur to walk upstairs, since he had a thing of importance to reveal to monsieur - one best said behind closed doors!"

I stared at her, my head humming like a top. Then, scrutinizingly, I looked about the court. The light in Miss Falconer's room had been extinguished. Did that have some significance? Was she lying perdue because these people had come? In the rooms opening from the west gallery above the street entrance I could see moving shadows. The gray car had arrived, and it bore three officers of France for passengers. What could this mean?

Of course, whoever had left the message had mistaken me for a confederate. I could not know any of the new arrivals; it was equally impossible that they could know me. None the less, with a slight, unaccustomed thrill of excitement, I resolved to accept the invitation as if in absolute good faith. It was a first-class chance to get inside those rooms, to use my eyes, to sound this affair a little, to learn whether these men were the girl's pursuers. As army officers they could scarcely be her accomplices. Would they forestall me by arresting her, by taking her back to Paris? It was astonishing how distasteful I found the idea of that.

I told madame that I thought I knew, now, who the gentlemen were. I climbed the west staircase with determination and knocked on the door of the first room that had a light. A voice from within, vaguely familiar, bade me enter, I did so immediately and closed the door.

Through an inner entrance I saw three men grouped about a table in the next room, all smoking cigarettes, all clad in horizon blue. They glanced up at me for a moment, and then, politely, they looked away. But a fourth man, who had stood beside them, came striding out to meet me, and I confronted Mr. John Van Blarcom face to face.

Officers fresh from the trenches have told me that one can lose through sheer accustomedness all horror at the grim sights of warfare, all consciousness of ear-splitting noises, all interest in gas and shrapnel and bursting shells. In the same way one can lose all capacity for astonishment, I suppose. I don't think I manifested much surprise at this unexpected meeting; and I heard myself remarking quite coolly that there had been a mistake, that I had been told downstairs that a friend of mine was here.

"That's right, Mr. Bayne," cut in Van Blarcom shortly. "I've been a friend of yours clear through, and I'm acting as one now. Just a minute, sir, please!"

He had shut the door between ourselves and the officers, and now he was drawing the shutters close. Coming back into the room, he seated himself, and motioned me toward a chair, which I didn't take. His authoritative manner was, I must say, not unimpressive. And he knew how to arrange a rather crude stage-setting; the room, with all air and sound excluded, seemed tense and breathless; the one dim candle on the table lent a certain solemnity to the scene.

"Look here, Mr. Bayne," he began bluffly, "last time you spoke to me you told me to - Well, we'll let bygones by bygones; I guess you remember what you said. You don't like me, and I'm not wasting any love on you; as far as you're personally concerned, I'd just as soon see you hang! But I've got to think of the United States. I'm in the service, and it doesn't do her any good to have her citizens get in bad with France."

Standing there, gazing at him with an air of bored inquiry, behind my mask of indifference I racked my brain. What did he want of me? What did he want of Miss Falconer? What was he doing in this military galley? Hopeless queries, without the key to the puzzle!

"Well?" I said.

"I don't ask you," he went on crisply, "what you're doing here -"

"You had better not!" I snapped. "What tomfoolery is this? Do you think you are a police officer heckling a crook? And why should you ask me such a question any more than I should ask you?"

He grinned meaningly.

"Well," he commented, "there might be reasons. I'm here on business, with papers in order, and three French officers to answer for me; but you're a kind of a funny person to make a bee-line for a place like Bleau. An inn like this doesn't seem your style, somehow. I'd say the Ritz was more your type. And while we're at it, did you go to the Paris *Prefecture* this morning, like all foreigners are told to, and show your passport, and get your police card? Have you got it with you? If you have you stepped pretty lively, considering you left Paris by three o'clock."

"If any one in authority asks me that," I said, "I'll answer him. I certainly don't propose to answer you." My arms were folded; I looked haughtily indifferent; but it was pure bluff. The only paper I had with me was my passport. What the dickens could I do if he turned nasty along such lines.

"As I was saying," he resumed, unruffled, "I'm not asking you why you're here - because I know. I've got to hand it to you that you're a dead-game sport. Most men's hair would have turned white at Gibraltar after the fuss you had. And here you are again - in the ring for all you're worth!"

"I suppose you mean something," I said wearily, "but it's too subtle and cryptic. Please use words of one syllable."

He nodded tolerantly. Leaning back, thumbs in his waistcoat-pockets, swelling visibly, he was an offensive picture of self-satisfaction and content.

"You can't get away with it, Mr. Bayne," he declared impressively. "You've taken on too much; I'm giving it to you straight. You can do a lot with money and good clothes, and being born a gentleman and acting like one, and having friends to help you; but you can't buck the French Government and the French army and the French police. In a little affair of this sort you wouldn't have a leg to stand on. Even your ambassador would turn you down cold. He wouldn't dare do anything else. This is the last call for dinner in the dining-car, for you. Last time I wanted to tell you the facts of the case you wouldn't listen. Will you listen now?"

I considered.

"Yes," I said, "I'll listen. Go ahead!"

He foundered for a moment, and then plunged in boldly.

"About this young lady who's brought you and me to Bleau. Oh, you needn't lift your eyebrows, much as to say, 'What young lady?' You know she's here, and I know it; and she knows I've come and has put her light out and is shaking in her shoes over there. I can swear to that. Well, I want to tell you I never started out to get her; I just stumbled across her on the steamer by a fluke. But I kept my eyes open and I saw a lot of things; and when I got to Paris to-day I told them at the *Prefecture*. You can see what they thought of the business by my being here. I wasn't keen to come. I've got my own work to do. But they want me to identify her; and they've sent three officers with me - not policemen, you'll notice, because this is an army matter, and before we make an end of it we'll be in the army zone."

I don't know just what he saw in my eyes; but it seemed to bother him. He fidgeted a little; as he approached the crucial point, his gaze evaded mine.

"Now, then, we'll come down to brass tacks, Mr. Bayne," said he. "I don't know what kind of story the girl told you; but I know it wasn't the truth or you wouldn't be here. That's sure. She's a German agent; she's come to get the Germans some papers that they want about as bad as anything under heaven. There's one man who tried the job already. He got killed for his pains; but he hid the papers before he died, and she knows where; and she's on her way to get them and carry the business through. I don't say she hasn't plenty of courage. Why, she's gone up against the whole of France; but I guess you're not very anxious to be mixed up in this underhand, spying sort of matter, eh?"

My hands were doubling themselves with automatic vigor. I wanted - consumedly - to knock the fellow down. However, I controlled myself.

"What's your offer?" I asked.

" It's this. " He was obviously relieved , positively

swelling in his tolerant, good-humored patronage. "I said once before I was sorry for you, and that still goes; we won't be hard on you if we have got the whip-hand, Mr. Bayne. You just stay in your room to-morrow until she's gone and we're gone, and you needn't be afraid your name will ever figure in this thing. I've made it all right with my friends in the next room. They know a pretty girl can fool a man sometimes, and they've got a soft spot for Americans, like all the Frenchies here. Take it from me, you'd better draw out quietly, instead of being arrested, tried, shot, or imprisoned maybe - or being sent home with an unproved charge hanging over you, and having all your friends fight shy of you as a suspected pro-German. Isn't that so?"

"You certainly," I agreed, "draw a most uninviting picture. I'll have to consider this, Mr. Van Blarcom, if you'll give me time?"

"Sure!" with his hearty response. "Take as long as you like to think it over; I know how you'll decide. You don't belong in a thing like this anyhow; you never did. It's bound to end in a nasty mess for all concerned. There's a train goes to Paris to-morrow morning at eleven. You just take it, sir, and forget this business, and you'll thank me all your life."

CHAPTER XV

GEORGES THE CHAUFFEUR

Upon descending to the courtyard, I took a seat on a bench beneath a vine-covered trellis. To stop here for a time, smoking, would seem a natural proceeding, and while I held such a post of recognizance nothing overt could transpire in the environs without my taking note of the fact. Enough had developed already, though, heaven was witness! I lit a cigarette and prepared for a resume.

Like a sleuth noting salient points, I glanced round the rectangular court. At my right, off the gallery, was Miss Falconer's room shrouded in darkness; at the left, up another flight of stairs, my own uninviting domain. The quarters of Van Blarcom and his uniformed friends opened from the gallery above the street passage, facing the main portion of the inn which sheltered the kitchen and *salle a manger*. Such was the simple, homely stage-setting. What of the play?

Bleau, I now felt tolerably sure, was merely a milestone on the route of Miss Falconer. Next morning, at sunrise probably, she would resume her journey for parts unknown. Would they arrest her before she left the inn or merely follow her? The latter, doubtless, since they asserted that she was on her way to get the papers that they wanted for France.

Upstairs in the room where Van Blarcom and I had held our conference the shutters had been reopened. There was just one light to be seen, a glowing point, which was obviously the tip of a cigar. If I was keeping vigil below, from above he returned the compliment; nor did he mean that I should hold any secret colloquy with the girl that night. I swore softly, but earnestly. Considering his rather decent attitude, his efforts from the very first to enlighten me as to the dangers I was running, it was odd that my detestation of the man was so thoroughly ingrained and so profound.

The mystery of the gray car had been solved with a vengeance. Instead of being freighted with accomplices, as I had at first thought possible, it had carried the representatives of justice, in the persons of three officers and my secret-service friend. A queer conjunction, that; but then, my ignorance of French methods was abysmal. Perhaps this was the usual mode of doing things in time of war.

Van Blarcom's explanation, though it made me furious, had brought conviction. There was a certain grim appositeness about it all. The night in New York, the events of the steamer, the unsatisfactory character of the girl's actions, all fitted neatly into the plan; and the mere personnel of the pursuing party was sufficient assurance, for French officers, as I well knew, were neither liars nor fools. Neither, I patriotically assumed, were the men of my country's secret-service, however humble their part as cogs in that great machinery, or however distasteful Mr. Van Blarcom, personally, might be to me. And finally, I could not deny that women, clever, well-born, and beautiful, had served as spies a thousand times in the world's history, urged to it by some sense of duty, some tie of blood.

Yes, that was it, I told myself in sudden pity, recalling how Miss Falconer had stood on the steps in her nurse's costume, straight and slender, her gray eyes full of fire, her face glowing like a rose. Perhaps she was of the enemy's country. Perhaps those she loved, those who made up her life, had set her feet in this path that she was treading. If she was a spy, - Lord! How the mere word hurt one! - it wasn't for ignoble motives; it wasn't for pay.

I came impulsively to the conclusion that there was just one course for my taking: to see her and to beg, bully, or wheedle from her the unvarnished truth. Then, if it was as I feared, she should go back to Paris if I had to carry her; she should accompany me to Bordeaux, and on the first steamer she should sail from France. Yes; and the army should have its papers, for she should tell me where they were hidden. Her work should end; but these men upstairs should not track her and trap her and drag her off to prison, perhaps to death.

There was danger in the plan, even if I should accomplish it. I should get myself into trouble, dark and deep. Well, if I had to languish behind bars for a while I could survive it. But she might not. As I thought of this I knew that I had made up my mind irrevocably.

It was a problem, nevertheless, to arrange an interview, with Van Blarcom sitting at his window, watching me like a lynx. I couldn't go up the stairs and batter on her door till she opened it; apart from the reception she would give me it would simply amount to making a present of my intentions to the men across the way. Yet who knew how long they would keep up their surveillance? Till I retired, probably! "I'd give something to choke you and be done with it!" was the benediction I wafted toward the sentinel above.

I was owning myself at my wit's end when a ray of hope was vouchsafed me. The kitchen door opened and let out a leather-clad figure which strode across the courtyard, lantern in hand, and let itself into the garage. Despite the dimness, I recognized Miss Falconer's chauffeur, the man she had addressed as Georges when they left the rue St.-Dominique. The very link I needed, provided I could get into communication with him in some unostentatious way.

I rose, stretched myself lazily, and began to pace the court. Perhaps a dozen times I crossed and recrossed it, each turn taking me past the garage and affording me a brief glance within. The chauffeur, coat flung aside, sleeves rolled up, was hard at work overhauling his engine, with an obvious view to efficiency upon the morrow. Up at the window I could see the glowing cigar-tip move now to this side, now to that. Not for an instant was Van Blarcom allowing me to escape from sight.

After taking one more turn I halted, yawned audibly for the sentry's benefit, and seated myself once more, this time on a bench by the door of the garage. Van Blarcom's cigar became stationary again. The chauffeur, who had satisfied himself as to the engine and was now passing critical fingers over the gashes in the tires, looked up at me casually and then resumed his work. Kneeling there, his tools about him, he was plainly visible in the light of the smoky lantern. He was a young man, twenty-three or-four perhaps, strongly built and obviously of French-peasant stock, with honest blue eyes and a face not unduly intelligent, but thoroughly frank and open in the cast. The actors in my drama, I had to own, were puzzling. This lad looked no more fitted than Miss Falconer for a treacherous role.

How theatrical it all was! And yet it had its zest. I confess I experienced a certain thrill, entirely new to me, as I bent forward with my arms on my knees and my head lowered to hide my face.

"*Attention, Georges!*" I muttered beneath my breath.

The chauffeur started, knocking a tool from the running-board beside him. His eyes, half-startled, half-fierce, fixed themselves on me; his hand went toward his pocket in a most significant way. In a minute he would be shooting me, I reflected grimly. And upstairs the very stillness of Van Blarcom shrieked suspicion; he could not have helped hearing the clatter that the falling tool had made.

"Don't be a fool," I muttered, low, but sharply. "I know where you and mademoiselle come from; I know she is upstairs now; if I wished you any harm I could have had the mayor and the gendarmes here an hour ago! Keep your head - we are being watched. Have a good look at me first if you feel you want to. Then take your hand off that revolver and pretend to go to work."

Throwing my head back, I began blowing clouds of smoke, wondering every instant whether a bullet would whiz through my brain. I could feel Georges' gaze upon me; I knew it was a critical moment. But as his kind are quick, shrewd judges of caste and character, I had my hopes.

They were justified; for presently I heard him draw a breath of relief. His hand came out of his pocket.

"Pardon, Monsieur," he whispered, and began a vigorous pretense of polishing the car.

Again I leaned forward to hide the fact that my lips were moving.

"When you speak to me, keep your head bent as I do."

"Monsieur, yes."

"Now listen. Men of the French army are here, with powers from the police. They accuse mademoiselle of serious things, of acts of treason, of being on her way to secure papers for the foes of France. They are watching. To-morrow, if she departs, they mean to follow and to arrest her when they have gained proof of what she is hunting."

"*Mon Dieu, Monsieur!* What shall I do?"

There was appeal in his voice. Convinced of my good faith, he was quite simply shifting the business to my shoulders - the French peasant trusting the man he ranked as of his master's class. And oddly enough I found myself responding as if to a trusted person. I smoked a little, wondering whether Van Blarcom could catch the faint mutter of our voices. Then I gave my orders in the same muffled tones:

"You will tell the servants that you wish to sleep here to-night, to watch the car. You will stay here very quietly until it is nearly dawn. Then you will creep to mademoiselle's door and whisper what I have told you and say that I beg her to meet me before those others have awakened at five o'clock in -"

Pondering a rendezvous, I hesitated. The room where I had dined, with its stone floor, its beamed ceiling, and dark panels, came first to my mind. I fancied, though, that some outdoor spot might be safer. I remembered opportunely that a passage led past this room, and that at its end I had glimpsed a little garden behind the inn.

"In the garden," I finished, and risked one straight look at him. "I can trust you, Georges?"

The young man's throat seemed to close.

"*Monsieur le duc* was my foster-brother, *Monsieur*," he whispered. "I would die for him."

Who the deuce *monsieur le duc* might be I did not tarry to discover. I had done all I could; the future was on the knees of the gods. Having smoked one more cigarette for the sake of verisimilitude, I rose, stretched myself ostentatiously, and crossed the courtyard to the stairs, where madame was descending. She had, she informed me, been preparing my bed.

"And I wish monsieur good repose," she ended volubly. "Hitherto, no Zeppelins have come to Bleau to disturb our dreams. Though, alas, who knows what they will do, now that we have lost our most gallant hero? Monsieur has heard of the Firefly of France, he who is missing?"

That name again! Odd how it seemed to pursue me.

"I believe I shall meet that fellow sometime if he's living," I reflected as I climbed the stairs.

In my room, my candle lighted, I resigned myself to a ghastly night. I don't like discomfort, though I can put up with it when I must. The bed looked as hard as nails; the bowl made cleanliness a duty, not a pleasure. And to think that I might have been sleeping in comfort at the Ritz!

Tossing from side to side, pounding a cast-iron pillow, I dozed through uneasy intervals, and woke with groans and starts. I could not rid myself of the sense of something ominous hanging over me. The gray car ramped through my dreams; so did Van Blarcom; and between sleeping and waking, I pictured my coming interview with the girl, her probable terror, the force and menaces I should have to use, our hurried flight.

At length I fell into a heavy, exhausted slumber, from which, toward morning I fancied, I sat up suddenly with the dazed impression of some sound echoing in my ears. Springing out of bed, I groped my way to the window. The galleries lay peaceful and empty in the moonlight, and down in the courtyard there was not the slightest sign of life.

I went back to bed in a state of jangled nerves. Again I dozed, and a dim light was creeping through the window when I woke. I looked out again.

"Hello!" I muttered, for though the hotel seemed wrapped in slumber, the door of the garage now stood ajar. Was it possible that Miss Falconer had stolen a march on me, that the automobile could have left the premises without my being roused? It was only four o'clock, but all wish for sleep had left me. I decided to investigate without any more ado.

I made the best toilet that cold water and a cracked mirror permitted, longing the while for a bath, for a breakfast tray, for a hundred civilized things. Taking my hat and coat, I went quietly down the staircase. The garage door beckoned me, and all unprepared, I walked into the tragedy of the affair.

In the dim place there were signs of a desperate struggle. The rugs and cushions of Miss Falconer's automobile were scattered far and wide. The gray car had vanished; and in the center of the floor was Georges, the chauffeur, lying on his back with arms extended, staring up at the ceiling with wide, unseeing blue eyes.

CHAPTER XVI

"I MUST GO ON"

Kneeling by the young man's side, I felt for his pulse; but the moment that my fingers touched his cold wrist I knew the truth. There flashed into my mind queerly, as things do at grim moments, an often-heard expression about rigor mortis setting in. With this poor fellow it had not started, but he was dead for all that. The most skilful surgeon in Europe could not have helped him now.

I never doubted that it was murder. The confusion of the garage was proof of it; and the instrument, once I looked about me, was not far to seek. Divided between rage, horror, and pity, I saw a sort of sharp stiletto suitable for use as a penknife or letter opener, which, after doing its work, had been cast upon the floor.

I remained on my knees beside the lad, smitten with a keen remorse. I knew no good of him; I had even suspected him; but he had an honest face. Why had I not kept watch all night? The instructions I had given, the plan I had thought so clever, might be responsible for the killing; it must have been some echo of the struggle that had roused me when I had wakened and glanced out and gone placidly back to sleep.

Marion Polk Angellotti

Had Van Blarcom caught our whispered colloquy, or surmised it? Helped by his precious colleagues, he must have taken Georges unprepared, throttled him to prevent his shouting, and ended his frantic struggles with one swift, ruthless blow. But why? What sort of soldiers could these be who wore the uniform of a brave, chivalrous country and yet did murder? What sort of mission were they bound upon that for no visible gain or motive they risked desperate work like this?

And the girl upstairs? The thought was like a knife thrust; it brought me to my feet, my heart pounding, my forehead cold and wet. I told myself that she must be safe, that wholesale killing could not be the aim of these wretches, that the gray automobile was not what our one-cent sheets in their tales of gunmen like to call a "murder car." But what did I know about it? I was in a funk, a funk of the bluest variety. In that one age-long moment I learned what sheer fright meant.

Without knowing how I got there, I found myself in the gallery. The doors that lined it were rickety and worm-eaten; I stared weakly at them. A mere twist of practised fingers, and they could be forced open by any one who cared to try. I thought I heard a faint breathing inside the girl's room, but I was not sure; I was too rattled. Very guardedly I knocked and got no answer. Then, in utter panic, I knocked louder, at risk of disturbing the whole house.

"Georges, *c'est vous*?" It was the drowsiest of murmurs, but few things have been so welcome to me in all my life.

" Yes , Mademoiselle. " Though my knees were

wobbling under me I summoned presence of mind to impersonate the poor huddled mass of flesh in the garage.

"*Attendez donc!*"

I could hear her stirring; she believed I had come with some summons, with some news. Well, it was imperative that I should see her. I waited obediently until the door swung open and revealed her in a loose robe of blue, with her hair in a ruddy mass about her shoulders and the sleep still lingering in her eyes.

"Mr. Bayne!"

Such was my relief at finding my fears uncalled for that I could have danced a breakdown on that crazy gallery, snapping my fingers in castanet fashion above my head. I had forgotten entirely the strained terms of our parting; but she remembered. A bright wave of scarlet ran over her face, her neck, her forehead. She gasped, clutched her robe about her, would have shut the door if I had not foreseen the strategic movement and inserted a foot in the diminishing crack, just in time.

"I beg your pardon," I began hastily. "I am really extremely sorry. But something has occurred that forces me to speak to you."

"There can be nothing that forces you to come here - nothing!" Her lips were trembling; her voice wavered; the apparent shamelessness of my behavior was driving her to the verge of tears. "Is there no place where I am safe from you? Mr. Bayne, how can you? I shan't listen to a single word while you keep your foot in the door!"

"And I can't take it away until you listen," I protested. "It is perfectly obvious that if I did, you would shut me out. But you can see for yourself that I'm not trying to force an entrance - and I wish that you would speak lower; if we waken anybody, there will be the mischief to pay."

My voice, I suppose, had an impatient note that was reassuring, or perhaps I looked encouragingly respectable, viewed at closer range. At any rate, she spoke less angrily, though she still stood erect and haughty.

"Well, what is it?" she asked, barring the opening with one slender arm.

"May I ask if you have had a message from me, Miss Falconer?"

"A message? Certainly not!" There was renewed suspicion in her voice.

"H'm." Then they had intercepted the man before he reached her. "I'm going to ask you to dress as quickly and quietly as possible and come downstairs. Don't stop in the court, and don't go near the garage, I beg of you. Just walk on past the *salle a manger* to the garden, and wait for me."

I expected exclamations, questions, indignant protests, anything but the sudden white calm that fell on her at my request.

"You mean," she whispered, "that something dreadful has happened. Is it about the - the men who came last night?"

"Yes. But please don't worry," I urged with false heartiness. "I'll explain when you come down." To cut the discussion short, I turned to go.

Once her door had closed, however, I halted at the staircase, retraced my steps, and, without hesitation, circled the gallery to the rooms of Mr. John Van Blarcom and his friends. I had had enough of uncertainties; henceforth I meant to deal with facts. It was barely possible that I was unjustly anathematizing these gentlemen, that, while they were peacefully sleeping, thieves had broken in below.

Two knocks, the first rather tentative, the second brisker, netting no response, I deliberately tried the knob and felt the door promptly yield to me; then, with equal deliberation, I dropped my hand into my pocket where my revolver lay. If some one sprang at me and tried to crack my head or stab me, - stabbing was popular hereabouts, - I was in a state of armed preparedness. But when I stepped inside I found an empty room, a bed in which no one had slept.

Grown brazen, I strode across to the inner door and opened it. More emptiness greeted me; the four men had plainly taken French leave in their gray car. It was strange that the hum of their departure had not roused me; they must, before starting the motor, have pushed their automobile from the courtyard and out of ear-shot down the street.

For a moment I stood in the deserted room, reflecting swiftly. The situation was desperate; in another hour the inn would be stirring, and Miss Falconer, I felt sure, could not afford to be found here when that came to pass. Murder investigations are searching things. All strangers beneath this roof would be interrogated narrowly. If any one had a secret, - and she certainly had several, - the chances were heavy that it would be dragged to light.

For some reason this prospect was unspeakably frightful to me. Under its spur I hatched the craziest scheme that man ever thought of, and took steps which, as I look back at them, seem almost beyond belief. I must get Miss Falconer off for Paris, I determined. And since it was possible that the villagers would see us leaving, she must appear to go, as she had come, with her chauffeur.

I descended, forthwith, to the garage where the murdered man was lying, shook out and folded the rugs that had been scattered in the struggle, picked up the cushions, and replaced them in the car. Then, borrowing a ruse from the enemy, I set the door wide open, and, puffing and panting, pushed the blue automobile into the courtyard, through the passage, and a considerable distance down the street.

What comes next, I ask no one to credit. Retrospectively, I myself have doubted it. It lives in my memory as a grisly nightmare rather than as a fact. To be brief, I returned to the scene of the crime, shut out any possible audience by closing the door, and disrobed hastily. Then I removed the leather costume of the victim, donned it, laced on his boots, which by good fortune were loose instead of tight, and, picking up his visored cap from the floor where it had fallen, stood forth to all seeming as genuine a member of the proletariate as ever wore goggles and held a wheel.

By this time my teeth were clenched as if in the throes of lockjaw. Had I paused to think for a single instant, all my nerve would have oozed away. But I had no time to spend on thought; I had to work on, to save Miss Falconer. The whole ghoulish business would be futile if the inn servants found the body. The mere flight of all the guests would certainly stir suspicion; let the murder transpire as well, and at once we should be pursued.

The garage, from the looks of it, was not often put to service. A dusty spot, festooned with cobwebs, it cried to the skies for brooms and mops. In the background, apparently undisturbed since the days of the First Empire, a great pile of straw mixed with junk of various kinds lay against the wall; and most reluctantly, my every fiber shrieking protest, I saw what use I might make of this debris - if I could.

"Go for it!" I told myself inexorably, but miserably. "It's not a question of liking it, you know. You've got to do it." Grimly I wrapped my discarded clothes about the poor chap's body, dragged it to the straw, and covered it from head to foot. By this action, I surmised, I was rendering myself a probable accessory and a certain suspect; but the one thing I really cared about was my last glimpse of that patient face.

"Sorry, old man," was all the apology I could muster. "And if I ever get a chance at the people who did it, you can count on me!"

With a sigh of complete exhaustion, I rose and looked about. All signs of the crime had been obliterated from the garage. "I must be crazy!" I thought, as the enormity of the thing rushed on me. "I wonder why I did it? And I wonder whether I can forget it some day - maybe after twenty years?"

As I opened the door to the garden the dim light was growing clearer. I was late; the girl, coated and hatted, ready for flitting, was already at the rendezvous. At sight of me in my leather togs she started backward; then, resolutely controlled, she drew herself up and faced me silently, her hands clutching at her furs, her lips a little apart.

"Won't you sit down?" I began lamely, indicating an iron bench. It was all so different from the interview I had planned last night! "I want to speak to you about your chauffeur, Miss Falconer. This morning I found him hurt - very badly hurt -"

She drove straight through my pretense.

"Not dead? Oh, Mr. Bayne, not dead?"

"Yes," I said gently. "He had been dead some time. I would have liked to take my chances with him; but I came too late. No, please!" She had moved forward, and I was barring her passage. "You mustn't go. You can't help him, and you wouldn't like the sight."

How black her eyes were in her white face!

"I don't understand," she faltered. "You mean that he was murdered? But who would have killed Georges?"

"The men who came last night - if you can call them men. At least, appearances point that way," I said.

"The men in the gray car?" She swayed a little.

"But why?"

"I'm afraid I can't tell you that." My tone was grim;
there were so many things about this matter that I
couldn't tell.

Her eyes flashed for an instant.

"But how cowardly, how cruel! He never hurt anyone;
he was just like a good watchdog, the truest, most
faithful soul! If they killed him they did it for some
deliberate purpose. And when I think that I brought
him here - oh, oh, Mr. Bayne -"

"Yes," I broke in hastily; "I should like to see them
boil in oil or fry on gridirons or something of the sort,
myself. But this is very serious; we must keep calm,
Miss Falconer. And I know you are going to help me.
You have such splendid self-control."

Though there were sobs in her throat, she pressed her
hands to her lips and stifled them. Only her pallor and
her wet lashes showed the horror and grief she felt. I
wanted desperately to comfort her, but there was no
time for it; and besides, who ever heard of a leather-
coated comforter in a kitchen garden at 5 A.M.?

"What I wanted to speak about," I went on rapidly,
"was our plans. This may prove a rather nasty mess,
I'm sorry to say. The French police, you know, are -
well, they're capable and very thorough; and since you
are here at the scene of a murder in an *infirmiere's*
costume, they will never rest till they have seen your
papers, learned your errand, asked you a hundred
things. Unless your replies are absolutely satisfactory,
the whole business will be - er - awkward for you. That

is why I put on these togs. Yes, I know it is ghastly," I owned as she shuddered. "And that is why I want to beg you, very seriously indeed, to let me drive you back to Paris and put you under your friends' protection. After that, of course, I'll return here to see the thing through and give my testimony about it all."

It was not going to be so simple, the course I had outlined airily. When I visioned myself explaining to a French *commissaire* why I had come to Bleau at all; why I had set up a false claim to be an artist, - for that circumstance was sure to leak out and look darkly incriminating, - and what had inspired me to take a murdered man's clothes and conceal his body, I can't pretend that I felt much zest. Still, if the police and the girl came together, worse would follow, I was certain; and it seemed like a real catastrophe when she slowly shook her head.

"I can't," she murmured. "Oh, it's kind of you, and I'm sorry; but I can't go back to Paris - not yet, Mr. Bayne. You won't understand, of course, but I left there to - to accomplish something. And since poor Georges can't help me now, I must go on - alone."

CHAPTER XVII

I BURN MY BRIDGES

If I live to be a hundred, and it is not improbable since I am healthy, I shall never forget that little garden at the inn at Bleau. It was a vegetable garden too, which is not in itself romantic. I recall vaguely that there were beds all about us, which in due course would doubtless sprout into rows of pale green objects - peas and artichokes, or beans and cabbages maybe; I don't know, I am sure. But then, there was the stream running just outside the wall of masonry; there was the sky, flushing with that faint, very delicate, very lovely pink that an early spring morning brings in France; there was the quaint building, wrapped up in slumber, beside us; and in the air a silent, fragrant dimness, the promise of the dawn.

And then there was the girl. I suppose that was the main thing. Not that I felt sentimental. I should have scouted the notion. If I meant to fall in love, - which, I should have said, I had no idea of doing, - I would certainly not begin the process in this unheard-of spot. No; it was simply that the whole business of caring for Miss Esme Falconer had suddenly devolved upon my shoulders; and that instead of my feeling bored, or annoyed, or exasperated at the prospect, my spirits rose inexplicably to face the need.

Here, if ever, was the time for the questions I had planned last evening. But I didn't ask them; I knew I should never ask them. In those few long unforgetable moments when I stood in the gallery and wondered whether she were living, my point of view had altered. I was through with suspecting her; I was prepared to laugh at evidence, however damning. As for the men in the gray car and their detailed accusations, I didn't give - well, a loud outcry in the infernal regions for them. I knew the standards of the land they served, and I had seen their work this morning. If they were French officers, I would do France a service by going after them with a gun.

The girl had sunk down on the ancient bench beside me. Her eyes, wide and distressed, yet resolute, went to my heart. Not a figure, I thought again, for this atmosphere of intrigue and secrecy and danger. Rather a girl, beautiful, brilliant, spirited, to be shielded from every jostle of existence; the sort of girl whom men hold it a test of manhood to protect from even the most passing discomfiture!

But time was moving apace. We must settle on something in short order. I spoke in the most matter-of-fact tones that I could summon, not, heaven knows, out of a feeling of levity concerning what had happened, but to try to lighten the grim business a degree or so and keep us sane.

"I think, Miss Falconer," I began, standing before her, "that we have got to thrash this matter out at last. You think I've behaved unspeakably, trailing you every-where, and I don't deny I have, according to your point of view. But the fact is, I didn't follow you to annoy you; I'm a half-way decent fellow. You have simply got to trust me until I've seen you through this tangle. After that, if you like you need never look at me again."

Her troubled eyes rested on me, half bewildered.

"Why, I'd forgotten all that," she murmured. "I do trust you, Mr. Bayne. Of course I must have misunderstood you to some way last evening, and I'm afraid I was disagreeable."

"Naturally. You had to be. Now, if that's all right and I'm forgiven, may I ask a question? About those men who arrived last night and apparently killed your chauffeur - can you guess who they are?"

"Yes," she faltered, looking down at the pebbled walk. "They must have been sent by the Government or the army or the police. If the French knew what I was doing, they wouldn't understand my motives. I've been afraid from the first that they would learn."

Another of my precious theories was going up in smoke. Not seeing why a set of bonafide officers should gratuitously murder a chauffeur, I had been wondering whether the quartet might not be impostors, tricked out in uniforms to which they had no claim. Still, of course, I couldn't judge. If she would only confide in me! I was fairly aching to help her; yet how could I, in this blindfold way?

"I don't wish to be impertinent," I ventured at length, meekly, "and I give you my word I'm not trying to find out anything you don't want me to. Only, assuming I've got some sense, - in case you care to be so amiable, - I'd like to put it at your service. Do you think you could give me just a vague outline of your plans?"

She looked at me in a piteous, uncertain manner. I braced myself for a "No." Then, suddenly, she seemed to decide to trust me - in sheer desperate loneliness, I dare say.

"I am going," she whispered, "to a village in the war zone - where there is a chateau. There are things in it - some papers; at least I believe there are. It is just a chance, just a forlorn hope; but it means all the world to certain people. I have to act in secret till I have succeeded, and then every one in France, every one on earth may know all that I have done!"

If I had not burned my bridges, this announcement might have worried me; it was too vague, and what little I grasped tallied startlingly with Van Blarcom's rigmarole. However, having bowed allegiance, I didn't blink an eyelid.

"Yes," I said encouragingly. "Is it very far?"

Her eyes went past me anxiously, watching the inn and its blank windows, as she fumbled in her coat and brought forth a motor map.

"Take it," she breathed, thrusting it toward me. "Look at it. Do you see? The route in red!"

As I realized the astounding thing I choked down an exclamation. There, beneath my finger, lay the village of Bleau, a tiny dot; and from it, straight into the war zone, the traced line ran through Le Moreau and Croix-le-Valois and St. Remilly; ran to - what was the name? I spelled it out: P-r-e-z-e-l-a-y.

Though it was early in the game to be a wet blanket, I found myself gasping.

"But," I protested weakly, "you can't do that! It's in the war country; it's forbidden territory. One has to have safe-conducts, *laissez-passers*, all sorts of documents to get into that part of France."

"I didn't come unprepared," she answered stubbornly. "Before I started I knew just what I should need. I can get as far as the hospital at Carrefonds; and Carrefonds is beyond Prezelay, ten miles nearer to the Front!"

"But - " The monosyllable was distinctly tactless.

She straightened, challenging me with brave, defiant eyes.

"I know," she flashed. "You mean it looks suspicious. Well, it does; and if I told you everything, it would look more suspicious still. You shouldn't have followed me; when they learn that we both spent the night here they will think you are my - my accomplice. The best advice I can give you, Mr. Bayne, is to go away."

"Perhaps we had better," I agreed stolidly. I had deserved the outburst. "Shall we be off at once, before the servants come downstairs?"

She drew back, her eyes widening.

"We?" she repeated.

"Naturally!" I replied, with some temper. "I *must* have disgusted you last night. What sort of a miserable, spineless, cowardly, caddish travesty of a man do you take me for, to think I would let you go alone?"

"Please don't joke," she urged. "It simply isn't possible. You would get into trouble with the French Government, and -"

"Do you know," I grinned, "it is rather exhilarating to snap one's fingers at governments? Just see what success I made of it with Great Britain and Italy, on the ship!"

"You don't realize what you are laughing at," she pleaded. "It is dangerous."

"I won't disgrace you. I seldom tremble visibly, Miss Falconer, though I often shake inside."

Her great gray eyes were glowing mistily.

"Mr. Bayne, this is splendid of you. I - I shall go on more bravely because you have been so kind. But I won't let you make such a sacrifice or mix in a thing that others may think disloyal, treacherous. You know how it looks. Why, on the steamer and on the way up to France and even last evening - you see I've guessed now why you followed me - you didn't trust me yourself."

"I know it," I confessed humbly. "I can't believe I was such an idiot. Somebody ought to perform a surgical operation on my brain. I apologize; I'm down in the dust; I feel like groveling. Won't you forgive me? I promise you won't have to do it twice."

This time it was she who said: " But - " and paused

uncertainly. I could see she was wavering, and I massed my horse, foot, and dragoons for the attack.

"You'll please consider me," I proclaimed firmly, "to be a tyrant. I am so much bigger than you are that you can't possibly drive me off. I don't mean to interfere or to ask questions, or to bother you. But I vow I'm coming with you if I cling to the running-board!"

Her lashes fluttered as she racked her brains for new protests.

"The car is a French make," she urged, - "which you couldn't drive -"

"I can drive any car with four wheels!" I exclaimed vaingloriously. "It's kismet, Miss Falconer; it's the hand of Providence, no less. Now, we'll leave these notes in the *salle a manger* to pay for our lodging, which would have been dear at twopence, and be off, if you please, for Prezelay."

She had yielded. We were standing side by side in the silence of the morning, the dimness fading round us, the air taking a golden tinge. My surroundings were plebeian; my costume was comic; yet I felt oddly uplifted.

"Jolly old garden, isn't it?" said I.

CHAPTER XVIII

IN THE HIGH GEAR

To pass straight from a humdrum, comfortable, conventionally ordered life into a career of insane adventure is a step that is radical; but it can be exhilarating, and I proved the fact that day. To dwell on present danger was to forget the past hour in the garage, which I had to forget or begin gibbering. Once committed to the adventure and away from the scene of the murder, I found a positive relief in facing the madness of the affair.

While the girl sat silent and listless, blotted against the cushions, rousing from her thoughts only to indicate the turns of the road, I had time for cogitation; and I began to feel like a man who has drunk freely of champagne. Hitherto I had been a law-abiding citizen. Now I had kicked over the traces. Like the distinguished fraternity that includes Raffles and Arsene Lupin, I should be "wanted" by the police, those good-natured, deferential beings so given to saluting and grinning, with whom, save for occasional episodes not unconnected with the speed laws, - Dunny says libelously that my progress in an automobile resembles a fabulous monster with a flying car for the head, a cloud of smokeand gasoline for the body, and a cohort of incensed motor-cycle men for the tail, - I had lived on the most cordial terms.

I was not certain whether they would accuse me of murder or espionage. There were pegs enough, undeniably, on which to hang either charge. Myself, I rather inclined to the latter; the case was so clear, so detailed! My rush from Paris to Bleau, - in order, no doubt, that I might at an unostentatious spot join forces with my confederate, Miss Falconer, whom I had been meeting at intervals ever since we left New York in company, - my behavior there, and the fashion in which we were vanishing should suffice to doom me as a spy.

When the French began tracing my movements, when they joined my present activities to the fact that only by the skin of my teeth had I escaped a charge of bringing German papers into Italy, there would be the devil to pay. I acknowledged it; then - really, this brand-new, unfounded, cast-iron trust of mine in Miss Falconer was changing me beyond recognition - I recalled the old recipe for the preparation of Welsh rabbit, and light-heartedly challenged the authorities to "catch me first." I had a disguise; if I bore any superior earmarks my leather coat obliterated them; and I could drive; even Dario Resta could not have sniffed at my technic. Better still, my French, learned even before my English, would not betray me. As nurse and as *mecanicien*, we stood a fair chance in our masquerade.

I might have to pay my shot, but I was enjoying it. This was a good world through which we were speeding; life was in the high gear to-day. The car purred beneath us like a splendid, harnessed tiger; the spring air was fresh and fragrant, the country charming, with here a forest, there a valley, farther off the tiled, colored roofs of some little town. Our road, like a white ribbon, wound itself out endlessly between stone walls or brown fields. In my content I forgot food and such prosaic details till I noticed that the girl looked pale.

"I say," I exclaimed remorsefully: "we've been omitting rolls and coffee! I'm going to get you some at the first town we pass."

"We are coming to a town now, to Le Moreau." She was looking anxious.

"Yes? I'm afraid I don't place it exactly. Ought I to?"

"It is the first town in the war zone. And - and our road passes through it."

"Oh!" I was enlightened. "Then they will probably ask to see our papers at the *octroi*?"

"Yes."

The car was eating up the smooth white road; I could see the little *octroi* building at the town boundary-line, and a group of gendarmes in readiness close by. It was a critical moment. Miss Falconer, I recalled, had said she could get through to Carrefonds; but glittering generalities were not likely to convince these sentries; one needed safe-conducts, passes, identity cards, and such concrete aids. She couldn't give a reasonable account of herself, I felt quite certain; and even if she did, how was she to account for me?

As I brought the car to a standstill, my conscience clamored, and my costume seemed to shriek incongruity from every seam. In this dilemma I trusted to sheer blind luck - a rather thrilling business. As a gray-headed sergeant stepped forward to welcome us, I looked him unfalteringly in the eye, though I wondered if he would not say:

"Monsieur, kindly remove that childish travesty with which you are trying to impose on justice. We know all about you. Your name is Devereux Bayne. You are a German agent and intriguer; you have smuggled papers; you have murdered a man and concealed his body. Unless you can give a satisfactory explanation of all your actions since leaving New York, your last hour has arrived!"

What he really said was:

"Mademoiselle's papers?" He spoke quite amiably, a catlike pretense, no doubt.

Miss Falconer was no longer looking anxious. Her hands were steady; she was even smiling as she produced two neat little packets that, on being unfolded, proved to have all the air of permits, *laissez-passers*, and police cards. Two nondescript photo-graphs, which might have represented almost any one, adorned them, and of these our sergeant made a perfunctory survey.

"Mademoiselle's name," he recited in a high singsong, "is Marie Le Clair. She is a nurse, on her way to the hospital at Carrefonds. And this is Jacques Carton, who is her chauffeur?"

A singularly stupid person, on the whole, he must have thought me, hardly fit to be trusted with so superb a car. My mouth, I fancy, was wide open; I can't swear that I wasn't pop-eyed. This last development had complete addled me. Marie Le Clair! Jacques Carton! Who were they?

"I wish," I remarked into the air as we drove on, "that some one would pinch me - hard."

She smiled faintly. Now it was over, she looked a little tremulous.

"Oh, no," she answered, "we were not dreaming. Poor Georges! I wish we were!"

Such was the incredible beginning of our adventure. And as it began, so it continued. We breakfasted at Le Moreau. Miss Falconer ate in the dining-room of the small hotel; I sought the kitchen and, warmed by our late success, I did not shrink from playing my role. Then we resumed our journey, and though we showed our papers twenty times at least as the control grew stricter, they were never challenged. I rubbed my eyes sometimes. Surely I should wake up presently! We couldn't be here in the forbidden region, in the war zone, plunging deeper every instant, in peril of our lives.

Yet the proof was thick about us. In the towns we passed we saw troops alight from the trains and enter them; we saw farewells and reunions, the latter sometimes tearful, but the former invariably brave. We saw *depots* where trucks and ambulances and commissary carts were filled, and canteens and soup kitchens where soldiers were being fed. At Croix-lc-Valois we saw the air turn black with the smoke of the munition factories that were working day and night. At St. Remilly above the towers of the old chateau we saw the Red Cross flying, and on the terraces the reclining figures of wounded men. It seemed impossible that sight-seers and pleasure-seekers had thronged along this road so lately. The signs of the Touring Club of France, posted at intervals, were survivals of an era that was now utterly gone.

With the coming of afternoon, the country grew still more beautiful. Orchards were thick about us, though the trees were leafless now. The little thatched cottages had odd fungi sprouting from their roofs like rosy mushrooms; the trees and streams had a silvery shimmer, like a Corot fairy-land.

Then, set like sign-posts of desolation in this loveliness, came the ravaged villages. We were on the soil where in the first month of the war the Germans had trod as conquerors, and where, step by step, the French had driven them back. We passed Cormizy, burnt to the ground to celebrate its taking; Le Remy, where the heroic mayor had died, transfixed by twenty bayonets; Bar-Villers, a group of ruined houses about a mourning, shattered church. It was the region where the Hun triumph had spoken aloud, unbridled. Miss Falconer sat white and silent as we drove through it; my hands tightened on the wheel.

We had lunched at Tolbiac, late and abominably. Then, leaving the highway, we had taken a country road. Two punctures befell us; once our carburetor betrayed the trust we placed in it. By the time these deficiencies were remedied I had collected dust and grease enough to look my part.

It had been, by and large, a singularly speechless day,

which my spasmodic efforts at entertainment had failed to cheer. The girl tried to respond, but her eyes were strained, eager, shadowed; her answers came at random. My talk, I suppose, teased her ears like the troublesome buzzing of a fly.

"She is thinking," I decided at last, "about those papers. Lord, if she doesn't find them she is going to take it hard!"

I left her in peace after that and drove the faster. Luck was with us! At the end of our journey everything would be all right.

As evening settled down on us the road grew increasingly lonely. Woods of oak-trees were about us, their trunks mossy, their branches lacing; on our left was a narrow river thick with rushes and smooth green stones. So rutty was the earth that our wheels sank into it and our engine labored. There was a charming sylvan look about the scenery; we seemed to be alone in the universe: I could not recall when we had last seen a peasant or passed a hut.

Suddenly I realized that there was a sound in the distance, not continuous, but steadily recurrent, a faint booming, I thought.

"What's that noise off yonder?" I asked, with one ear cocked toward the east.

Miss Falconer roused herself.

"It is the cannonading," she answered. "We have come a long way, Mr. Bayne. In two hours - in less than that - we could drive to the Front. And see!"

The dark was coming fast; a crimson sunset was reddening the river. A little below us on the opposite bank, I saw what had been a village once upon a time. But some agency of destruction had done its work there; blackened spaces and heaped stones and the shells of dwellings rose tier on tier among trees that seemed trying to hide them; only on the crest of the bank, overlooking the wreck like a gloomy sentinel, one building loomed intact, a dark, scarred, frowning castle with medieval walls and towers. I stared at the scene of desolation.

"The Germans again!" I said.

"Yes," the girl assented, gazing across the water. "They came here at the beginning of the war. They burned the houses and the huts and the little church with the image of the Virgin and the tomb of the old constable - all Prezelay except the chateau; and they only left that standing to give their officers a home."

With an automatic action of feet and fingers, I stopped the car. Here was the town that she had shown me on the map that morning when we sat like a pair of whispering conspirators in the garden of the Three Kings. The obstacles which had seemed so great had melted away before us. This ruined village, this heap of stones cross the river, was our goal, the key to our mystery, the last scene of our drama - Prezelay.

CHAPTER XIX

THE CASTLE AT PREZELAY

In the midst of my triumph, which was as intense as if I myself, instead of pure luck, had engineered our journey, I became aware of a tiny qualm as I sat gazing across the stream. Perhaps the gathering night affected me, or the air, which was growing chilly, or the remnants of the village, which were cheerless, to say the least. But that castle, perched so darkly on its crag, with a strip of blood-red sky framing it, was at the heart of my feeling. If it had been a nice, worldly-looking, well-kept chateau, with poplared walks and a formal garden, I should have welcomed it with open arms; but it wasn't, decidedly! It was the threatening age-blackened sort of place that inevitably suggests Fulc of Anjou, strongholds on the Loire, marauding barons, and the good old days with their concomitants of rapine and robbery and death.

It was picturesque, but it was intensely gloomy; the proper spot for a catastrophe rather than a happy denouement. I was not impressionable, of course; but now that I thought of it, our jaunt had been going with a smoothness almost ominous. Could one expect such clock-like regularity to run forever without a break?

Take the utter disappearance of the gray car, for

instance. That had seemed to me reassuring; but was it? Those four men had cared enough about Miss Falconer's movements to involve themselves in a murder. Why, then, should they have given up the chase in so mysterious a way?

And the girl herself! When I looked at her I felt horribly worried. She was shivering through her furs; yet it was not with the cold, I felt quite sure. With her hands clasped, she sat staring at that confounded castle with a look of actual hunger. She cared too much about this thing; she couldn't stand a great deal more.

Well, she wouldn't have to, I concluded, my brief misgivings fading. We were out of the woods; another hour would see the business closed. As for the men in the car, they were victims of their guilty consciences, were no doubt in full flight or hiding somewhere in terror of the law.

At any rate, there was no point in my sitting here like a graven image; so I roused myself and wrapped the rugs closer about the girl.

"I'm to drive to the chateau?" I inquired with recovered cheerfulness. I had to repeat the words before they broke her trance.

"Yes," she answered. Suddenly, impulsively, she turned toward me, her face almost feverish, her eyes astonishingly large and bright. "I haven't told you much," she acknowledged tremulously; "but you won't think that I don't trust you. It is only that I couldn't talk of it and keep my courage; and I must keep it a little longer - until we know the truth."

"That's quite all right, Miss Falconer." I was switching on the lamps. Then I extinguished them; their clear acetylene glare seemed almost weirdly out of place. "We can muddle along without any lights. Not much traffic here," I muttered. I had a feeling, anyhow, that unostentatiousness of approach might not be bad.

There was intense silence about us; not even a breeze was stirring. A thin crescent moon was out, silvering the river and the trees. The road was atrocious; on one dark stretch the car, rocking into a rut, jolted us viciously and brought my teeth together on the tip of my tongue.

"Sorry," I gasped, between humiliation and pain.

With the silence and the dimness, we were like ghosts, the car like a phantom. An old stone bridge seemed to beckon us, and we crossed to the other side. There, at Miss Falconer's gesture, I drew the automobile off the road at the edge of the town, halted it beneath some trees, and helped her to alight. We started up the hill together without a word.

Two ghosts! More and more, as we climbed through the wreck and desolation, that was what we seemed. The road was choked with stones between which the grass was sprouting; there was nothing left of the little church save a single pointed shaft. We climbed rapidly, the girl always gazing up at the castle with that same feverish eagerness. She had forgotten, I think, that I was there.

At last we were coming to the hilltop and the chateau. Rather breathless, I studied its looming walls, its turrets, its three round towers. It looked dark and inexplicably menacing, but I had recovered my form and could defy it. When we halted at a great iron-studded oak gate and Miss Falconer pulled the bell-rope, I was astonished. It had not occurred to me that the castle would be more inhabited than the town.

Nor was it, apparently; for no one answered its summons, though I could hear the bell jingling faintly somewhere within. Miss Falconer rang a second time, then a third; her face shone white in the moonlight; she was growing anxious.

"Did you think," I ventured finally, "that there was some one here?"

"Yes; Marie-Jeanne," she answered, listening intently. Then she roused herself. "I mean the *gardienne*. She never left, not even when the Germans came. They made her cook for them; she said she had been born in the keeper's lodge, and her grandfather before her, and that she would rather die at Prezelay than go to any other place. But of course she may have walked down the river for the evening. Her son's wife is at Santierre, two miles off. She may be there."

"That's it," I agreed hastily, the more hastily because I doubted. "She's sitting over a fire, toasting her toes, and gossiping and having a cup of tea, or whatever people like that use for an equivalent in these parts." I suppressed the unwelcome thought that a woman living here alone ran a first-rate chance of getting her throat cut by strolling vagrants. "Shall we have to wait until she comes back?" I asked. "Then let's sit down. I choose this stone!"

On my last word, however, something surprising

happened. Miss Falconer, in her impatience, put a hand on the bolt of the gate, shook it, and raised it, and, lo and behold! the oak frame swung open. Before I quite realized the situation, we were inside, in a square courtyard, with the *gardienne's* lodge at the right of us, impenetrably barred and shuttered, and before us the portal of the castle, surmounted with quaint stone carvings of men in armor riding prancing steeds. The court, as revealed by the moonlight, was intact, but neglected. Weeds were sprouting between the square blocks of stone that paved it, and in the center a wide circular space, charred and blackened, showed where the German sentries had built their fires. It was not cheerful, nor was it homey. I scarcely blamed Marie-Jeanne for flitting. The faint sound of the cannonading had begun again in the distance, but otherwise the place was as silent as a tomb.

"It seems strange!" Miss Falconer murmured, looking about in puzzled fashion. "Why in the world should she have left the gate open in this careless way? Of course there is nothing here for thieves; the Germans saw to that; but still, as keeper - Oh, well, it doesn't matter. It saves us from waiting till she comes home."

As I followed her toward the castle entrance, she opened the bag she carried, and produced a candle, which I hastened to take and light. I nearly said, "The latest thing in the housebreaking line, madame, is electric torches, not tapers"; but I decided not to. After all, perhaps we were housebreakers. How could I tell?

Hot candle wax splashed my fingers and scorched them, but I scarcely noticed. My sense of high-gear adventure had reached its zenith now. There was something thrilling, something stimulating in this stealthy night entrance into a deserted castle. It was an experience, at all events; there was no *concierge* to stump before one through dim passages and up winding staircases; no flood of dates and names and anecdotes poured inexorably into one's bored ears to insure a *douceur* when the tour of the chateau should be done.

The door - faithless Marie-Jeanne! - opened as readily as the outer gate. We were entering. I glimpsed in a dim vista a superb Gothic hall of magnificent archi-tecture and most imposing proportions, arched and carved and stretching off with apparent endlessness into the gloom. Holding up my light, I scanned the place with growing interest. It had not been demolished, but neither had it been spared. The furniture was gone, save for a few scattered chairs and a table; the walls were defaced with cartoons and scrawled inscriptions; the floor was stained, and littered with empty bottles and broken plates. From the chimney-place - a medieval-art jewel topped with carved and colored enamels - pieces had been hacked away by some deliberately destructive hand. I glanced at Miss Falconer, whose eyes had been following mine.

"They tore down the tapestries," she said beneath her breath. "They slashed the old portraits with their swords and broke the windows and took away the statues and candlesticks and plate. They cut up the furniture and had it used for fire-wood; and the German captain and his officers had a feast here and drank to the fall of Paris and ordered their soldiers to burn the village to the ground. Oh, I don't like the place any more; too much has happened. And - and I don't like Marie-Jeanne's not being here, Mr. Bayne. I feel as if there were something wrong about it. I believe I am a little - just a little afraid!"

"Come, now, you don't expect me to believe that, do you?" I countered promptly. "Because I won't. Why, it's your pluck that has kept me up all day. Just the same, on general principles, I'll take a look round if you'll allow me. Here's a chair, and if you will rest a minute, I'll guarantee to find out."

The chair I mentioned was standing near the chimney, and as I spoke I walked over to it and started to spin it round. It resisted me heavily; I bent over it, lifting my candle. Then I uttered an exclamation, stood petrified, and stared.

In the chair, concealed from us until now by the high carved back of wood, was something which at first looked like a huddled mass of garments, but which on closer scrutiny resolved itself into a woman in a striped dress, an apron, and a pair of heavy shoes. There was a cut on her cheek, a bruise on her forehead. Locks of graying hair straggled from beneath her disarranged white cap, and she glared at me from a lean, sallow face with a pair of terrified eyes.

She must be dead, I thought. No living woman could sit so still and stare so wildly. The scene in the inn garage rushed back upon me, and I must say that my blood turned cold. But she was alive, I saw now; she was certainly breathing. And an instant later I realized why she stayed so immobile; she was bound hand and foot to the chair she sat in, and a colored handkerchief, her own doubtless, had been twisted across her mouth to form a gag.

"I think," I head myself saying, "that we have been maligning Marie-Jeanne."

A choked, frightened cry from Miss Falconer made me wheel about sharply, to find her staring not a me, but at the further wall. Prepared now for anything under heaven, I followed her gaze. Above us, circling the whole hall, there ran a gallery from which at a distance of some fifteen feet from where we stood a wide stone staircase descended; and half-way down this, as motionless as statues, as indistinct as shadows, I saw four men in the uniform of officers of France.

For an uncanny moment I wondered whether they were specters. For a stupid one, I thought they might be people whom the girl had come here to meet. Still, if they were, she wouldn't be looking at them in this paralyzed fashion. I could not see them plainly, - but they must be the men from Bleau.

"Well, Mr. Bayne," the foremost was asking, "did you think we had deserted you? Not a bit of it! We came on ahead and rang up the old woman there and commandeered her keys. We've been killing time here for a good half hour, waiting for you. You must have had tire trouble. And you don't seem very pleased to see us now that you've come - eh, what?"

At Bleau the previous night, I was recalling dazedly, there had been only three men wearing the horizon blue. Who was this fourth figure, who knew my name and spoke such colloquial English? I raised my candle as high as possible and scanned him. Then I stood transfixed.

" Van Blarcom! " I gasped. "And in a uniform, by all

that's holy!"

He grinned.

"No. You haven't got that quite right," he told me. "What's the use keeping up the game now that we're here, all friends together? My name isn't Van Blarcom. It's Franz von Blenheim, Mr. Bayne.

CHAPTER XX

INTRODUCING HERR FRANZ VON BLENHEIM

The words of Franz von Blenheim seemed to fill the hall and reecho from the walls and arches, deafening me, leaving me stunned as if by an earthquake or by a flash of lightning from clear skies. Yet I never though of doubting them. Comatose as my state was, slowly as my brain was working, I recognized vaguely how many features of the mystery, both past and present, these words explained.

It was odd, but never once had it occurred to me that Van Blarcom might be a German. He himself, I began to realize, had taken care of that. With considerable acumen he had filled every one of our brief interviews with vigorous denunciations of somebody else, dark hints as to intrigues that surrounded me and might enmesh me, and solemn warnings and prudent counsels, which had brilliantly served his turn. He had kept me so busy suspecting Miss Falconer - at the thought I could have beaten my head against the wall in token of my abject shame - that my doubts had never glanced in his direction; a most humiliating confession, since I couldn't deny, reviewing the past in this new light, that circumstances had afforded me every opportunity to guess the truth.

Marion Polk Angellotti

There was no time, however, for dwelling on my deficiencies. The next half hour would be an uncommonly lively one, I felt quite sure. I might call the thing bizarre, fantastic; I might dub it an extravaganza; the fact remained that I was shut up in this lonely spot with four entirely able-bodied Germans and must match wits with them over some affair that apparently was of international consequence; for if it had been a twopenny business, Herr von Blenheim, the star agent of the kaiser, would never have thought it worth his pains.

With all my fighting spirit rising to meet the odds against us, I cast a speculative eye over the Teutons, who had now dissolved their group. Van Blarcom himself - Blenheim, rather - descended in a leisurely fashion while one of his friends, remaining on the staircase, fixed me with a look of intentness almost ominous and the other two placed themselves as if casually before the door. They were stalwart, well set-up men, I acknowledged as I surveyed them. Though not bad at what our French friends call *la boxe*, I was outnumbered. It was obviously a case of strategy - but of what sort?

A much defaced table, flanked with a few battered chairs, stood near me, and with a premonition that I should want two hands presently, I set my candle there. Then I drew a chair forward and turned to the girl with outward coolness.

"Please sit down, Miss Falconer," I invited. I wanted time.

She inclined her head and obeyed me very quietly. She was not afraid; I saw it with a rush of pride. As she sat erect, her head thrown back, on gloved hand resting on the table, she was a picture of spirit and steadiness and courage. If I had needed strength I should have found it in the fact that her eyes, oddly darkened as always when her errand was threatened did not rest on our captors, but turned toward me.

"We'll all sit down," Franz von Blenheim agreed most amiably. It evidently amused him to retain the late Mr. Van Blarcom's dialect and air. "We can fix this business up in no time; so why not be sociable?" He strolled to a chair and sank into it and motioned me to do the same.

"Thanks," I returned, not complying. "If you don't mind, I'd like first to untie that woman. I confess to a queer sort of prejudice against seeing women bound and gagged. In fact I feel so strongly on the subject that it might spoil our whole conference for me." I took a step toward the shadowy figure of Marie-Jeanne.

Blenheim did not move, but his eyes seemed to narrow and darken.

"Just leave her alone for the present. She is too fond of shrieking - might interrupt our argument," he declared. "And see here, Mr. Bayne," he added, warned by my manner, "I want to call your attention to the gentleman on the stairs, my friend Schwartzmann. He's a crack shot, none better, and he has got you covered. Hadn't you better sit down and have a friendly chat?"

Though the stairs were dim, I could see something glittering in the hand of the person mentioned, who was impersonating for the evening a dashing young captain of the general staff. My fingers strayed toward my pocket and my own revolver. Then I pried them away, temporarily, and took a provisional seat.

"That's sensible," Franz von Blenheim approved me blandly. "Now, Miss Falconer, you know what I'm here for, isn't that so? Just hand me those papers and you'll be as free as air. I'll take myself off; you'll never see me again probably. That's a fair bargain, isn't it? What do you say?"

I was sitting close to the girl, so close that her soft furs brushed me and I could feel the flutter of her breath against my cheek. At Blenheim's proposition I glanced at her. She was measuring him steadily. Then she looked at me, and her eyes seemed to hold some message that I could not read.

"Perhaps, Miss Falconer," I interposed, "you have not quite grasped the situation." I was sparring for time; she wanted to convey something to me, I was sure. "It is rather complicated. This gentleman has turned out to be a well-known agent of the kaiser. He was traveling on the *Re d'Italia*, I gather, on a forged passport, and had helped himself to my baggage as the most convenient way of smuggling some papers to the other side."

He grinned assentingly.

"You owe me one for that," he owned. "You see, it was my second trip on that line, and I thought they might have me spotted; I had a lot of things to carry home, - reports, information, confidential letters, and I concluded they would be safer with a nice, innocent young man like you. It didn't work, as things went. It was just a little too clever. But if you hadn't mixed yourself up with this young lady, and tossed packages overboard for her under the noses of the stewards, and got yourself suspected and your baggage searched, I should have turned the trick!"

His share in the tangled episode on board the steamer was unfolding. I understood now why he had sprung to my rescue in the salon when I was accused. Naturally he had not wanted my traps searched, considering what was in them.

"As you say, you were a little too clever," I agreed.

His eyes glinted viciously.

"Well, it's no use crying over spilt milk," he retorted; "and besides, the papers you are going to hand me to-night will even up the score. It was a piece of luck, my running across Miss Falconer on the liner. Of course the minute I heard her name I knew what she was crossing for." The dickens he did! "All I had to do was to follow her, and by the time we reached Bleau I had guessed enough to come ahead of her. But I'll admit, Mr. Bayne, now it's all over, it made me nervous to have you popping up at every turn! I began to think that you suspected me - that you were trailing me. If you had, you know, I shouldn't have stood a chance on earth. You could have said a word to the first gendarme you met and had me laid by the heels and ended it. That was why I kept warning you off. But I needn't have worried. You drank in everything I told you as innocent as a babe!"

If he wanted revenge for my last remark, he had it. I looked at the girl beside me, so watchfully composed and fearless, then at the fixed, terrified glare of the motionless Marie-Jeanne. With a little rudimentary intelligence on my part this situation would have been spared us.

"Yes," I acknowledged bitterly; "I did."

"Except for that," he grinned, "it went like clockwork. There wasn't even enough danger in the thing to give it spice. Do you know, there isn't a capital in Europe where I can't get disguises, money, passports within twelve hours if I want them. Oh, you have a bit to learn about us, you people on the other side! I've crossed the ocean four times since the war started; I've been in London, Rome, Paris, Petrograd - pretty much every-where. I'm getting homesick, though. The *laissez-passer* I've picked up, or forged, no matter which, takes me straight through to the Front; and I've got friends even in the trenches. Before the Frenchies know it I'll be across no-man's-land and inside the German lines!"

For a moment, as I listened, I was dangerously near admiring him. He was certainly exaggerating; but it couldn't all be brag. The life of this spy of the first water, of international fame, must be rather marvelous; to defy one's enemies with success, to journey calmly through their capitals, to stroll undetected among their agents of justice - were not things any fool could do. He carried his life in his hand, this Franz von Blenheim. He had courage; he even had genius along his special lines. His impersonation on the liner, shrewd, slangy, coarse-grained, patronizing, had been a triumph. Then, suddenly, I remembered a murdered boy beside whom I had knelt that morning, and my brief flicker of homage died.

"You think I can't do it, eh?" He had misinterpreted my expression. "Well, let me tell you I did just a year ago and got over without a scratch. To get across no-man's-land you have to play dead, as you Yankees put it; you lie flat on the ground and pull yourself forward a foot at a time and keep your eye on the search-lights so that when they come your way you can drop on your face and lie like a corpse until they move on. It's not pleasant, of course; but in this game we take our chances. And now I think I'll be claiming my winnings if you please."

I straightened in my chair, recognizing a crisis. With his last phrase he had shed the bearing of Mr. John Van Blarcom, and from the disguise all in an instant there emerged the Prussian, insolent, overbearing, fixing us with a look of challenge, and addressing us with crisp command. No; the kaiser's agent was not a figure of romance or of adventure. He was a force as able, as ruthless, as cruel as the land he served.

"Miss Falconer," he demanded briefly, "where are those papers? I am not to be played with, I assure you. If you think I am, just recall this morning, and your chauffeur. We didn't kill him for the pleasure of it; he had his chance as you have. But when we went for our car he was there in the garage, sleeping; he seemed to think we had designs on him, and tried to rouse the inn."

"Do you call that an excuse for a murder?" I exclaimed. "You cold-blooded villain!"

"I don't make excuses." His voice was hard and arrogant. "I am calling the matter to your notice as a kind warning, Mr. Bayne. You said a little while ago that to see a woman gagged and bound distressed you. Well, unless I have those papers within five minutes, you will see something worse than that!"

At the moment what I saw was red. There was something beating in my throat, choking me; I knew neither myself nor the primitive impulses I felt.

"If you lay a finger on Miss Falconer," I heard myself saying slowly, "I swear I'll kill you."

Then through the crimson mist that enveloped me I saw Blenheim laugh.

"Come, Mr. Bayne," he taunted me, "remember our friend Schwartzmann. This is your business, Miss Falconer, I take it. What are you going to do?"

The girl flung her head back, and her eyes blazed as she answered him.

"You can torture me," she said scornfully. "You can kill me. But I will never give you the papers; you may be sure of that."

CHAPTER XXI

IN THE DARK

I thought of a number of things in the ensuing thirty seconds, but they all narrowed down swiftly to a mere thankfulness that I had been born. Suppose I hadn't; or suppose I had not happened to stop at the St. Ives Hotel and sail on the *Re d'Italia*; or that I had remained in Rome with Jack Herriott instead of hurrying on to Paris; or had let my quest of the girl end in the rue St.-Dominique instead of trailing her to Bleau. If one of these links had been omitted, the chain of circumstance would have been broken, and Miss Falconer would have sat here confronting these four men alone.

It was extremely hard for me to believe that the scene was genuine. The dark hall, the one wavering, flickering candle lighting only the immediate area of our conference, the bound woman in the chair, the watchful attitude of our captors. Mr. Schwartzmann's ready weapon - all were the sort of thing that does not happen to people in our prosaic day and age. It was like an old-time romantic drama; I felt inadequate, cast for the hero. I might have been Francois Villon, or some such Sothern-like incarnation, for all the civilized resources that I could summon. There were no bells here to be rung for servants, no telephones to be utilized, no police station round the corner from

Marion Polk Angellotti

which to commandeer prompt aid.

The most alarming feature of the affair, however, was the manner of Franz von Blenheim, which was not so much melodramatic as businesslike and hard. At Miss Falconer's defiance he looked her up and down quite coolly. Then, turning in his seat, he began giving orders to his men.

"Schwartzmann," ran the first of these, "I want you to watch this gentleman. He will probably make some movement presently; if he does, you are to fire, and not to miss. And you" - he turned to the men by the door - "pile some wood in the chimney-place and light it. There are some sticks over yonder, - but if you don't find enough, break up a chair. Then when you get a good blaze, heat me one of the fire-irons. Heat it red-hot. And be quick! We are wasting time!"

The color was leaving the girl's cheeks, but she sat even straighter, prouder. As for me, for one instant I experienced a blessed relief. I had been right; it was all impossible. One didn't talk seriously of red-hot irons.

"You must think you are King John," I laughed. "But you're overplaying. Don't worry, Miss Falconer; he won't touch you. There are things that men don't do."

He looked at me, not angrily, not in resentment, but in pure contempt; and I remembered. There were people, hundreds of them, in the burning villages of Belgium, in the ravaged lands of northern France, who had once felt the same assurance that certain things couldn't be done and had learned that they could. I glanced at the men who were piling wood on the hearth, at their sullen blue eyes, their air of rather stupid arrogance. I had walked, it seemed, into a nightmare; but then, so had the world.

"This isn't a tea party, Mr. Bayne," said Franz von Blenheim. "It is war. Those papers belong to my government and they are going back. I shall stop at nothing, nothing on earth, to get them; so if you have any influence with this young lady, you had better use it now."

"I am not afraid." The girl's voice was unshaken, bless her. "I said you could kill me - and I meant it. But I will not tell."

"And I will not kill you, Miss Falconer." The German's tones were level, and his eyes, as they dwelt steadily on her, were as hard and cold as steel. "I don't want you dead; I want you living, with a tongue and using it; and you will use it. You talk bravely, but you have no conception - how should you have? - of physical pain. When that iron is red-hot, if you have not spoken, I shall hold it to your arm and press it -"

"Damn you!" The cry was wrenched out of me. "Not while I am here!"

"You will be here, Mr. Bayne, just so long as it suits me." A sort of cold ferocity was growing in Blenheim's tones. "And you have yourself to thank for your position, let me remind you; you would thrust yourself in. I don't know what you are doing in the business - a ridiculous mountebank in a leather cap and coat! It's a way you Yankees have, meddling in things that don't concern you. You seem to think that you have special rights under Providence, that you own everything in the universe, even to the high seas. Well, we'll settle with your country for its munitions and its notes and its driveling talk about atrocities a little later, when we have finished up the Allies. And I'll deal with you to-night if you dare to lift a hand."

There seemed only one answer possible, and my muscles were stiffening for it when suddenly Miss Falconer's handkerchief, a mere wisp of linen which she had been clenching between her fingers, dropped to the floor. With a purely automatic movement, I bent to recover it for her; she leaned down to receive it. Her pale face and lovely dilated eyes were close to me for a fleeting second, and though her lips did not move, I seemed to catch the merest breath, the faintest gossamer whisper that said:

"The stairs!"

Blenheim's gaze, full of suspicion, was upon us as we straightened, but he could not possibly have heard anything; I had barely heard myself. I racked my brains. The stairs! But the man Schwartzmann was guarding them with his revolver. I couldn't imagine what she meant; and then suddenly I knew.

Throughout the entire scene, whenever I had glanced at her, I had noticed the steady way in which her look met mine and then turned aside. It had seemed almost like a signal or a message she was trying to give me. And which way had her eyes always gone? Why, down the hall!

I looked in that direction and felt my heart leap up exultantly. Perhaps twenty feet from us, just where the radius of the candle-light merged off into the darkness, I glimpsed what seemed the merest ghost of a circular stone staircase, carved and sculptured cunningly, like lacy foam. Up into the dusk it wound, to the gallery, and to a door. Behold our objective! I wasted no precious time in pondering the whys and the wherefores. At any rate, once inside with the bolts shot we could count on a breathing-space.

I cast a final glance at Blenheim where he lolled across the table, and at the shadowy menacing figure of the armed sentinel on the stairs. The men at the hearth had piled their wood and were bending forward to light it.

"Be ready, please!" I said to the girl, aloud.

As I spoke I bent forward, seized the table by its legs, and raised it, and concentrated all the wrath, resentment and detestation that had boiled in me for half an hour into the force with which I dashed it forward against Blenheim's face. He grunted profoundly as it struck him. Toppling over with a crash, he rolled upon the floor. The candle, falling, extinguished itself promptly, and we were left standing in a hall as black as ink.

Simultaneously with the blow I had struck there came a spit of flame from the staircase, a sharp crack, and as I ducked hastily a bullet spurted past me, within three inches of my head. Miss Falconer was beside me. Together we retreated, while a second shot, which this time went wide, struck the wall beyond us and proved that Schwartzmann, though handicapped, was not giving up the fight.

So far things had gone better than I had dared to think was possible. Now, however, they took a sudden and most unwelcome turn. One of the men by the chimney-place must have wasted no time in leaping for me; for at this instant, quite without warning, he catapulted on me through the darkness with the force of a battering-ram.

The table, which I still held clutched with a view to emergencies, broke the force of his onslaught. He reeled, stumbled, and collapsed on his knees. However, he was lacking neither in Teutonic efficiency nor in resource. Putting out a prompt hand, he seized my ankle and jerked my foot from under me; the table dropped from my grasp with a splintering uproar, and I fell.

Before I could recover myself my enemy had rolled on top of me, and I felt his fingers at my throat as he clamored in German for a light. He was a heavy man; his bulk was paralyzing; but I stiffened every muscle. With a mighty heave I turned half over, rose on my elbow, and delivered a blow at what, I fondly hoped, might prove the point of his chin.

Dark as it was, I had made no miscalculation. He dropped on me once again, but this time as an inert mass. Burrowing out from under him, I sprang to my feet aglow with triumph - and found myself in the clutch of the second gentleman from the chimney-place, who apparently had come hotfoot to his comrade's aid.

I was fairly caught. His arms went round me like steel girders, pinioning mine to my sides before I knew what he was about. In sheer desperation I summoned all the strength I possessed and a little more. Ah! I had wrenched my right arm loose; now we should see! I raised it and managed, despite the close quarters at which we were contending, to plant a series of crashing blows on my adversary's face.

The fellow, I must say, bore up pluckily beneath the punishment. He hung on. There would be a light in a moment, he was doubtless thinking, and when once that came to pass, it would be all over with me. But at my fifth blow he wavered groggily, and at my sixth, endurance failed him. He groaned softly. Then his grasp relaxed, and he collapsed quietly on the floor.

Throughout the swift march of these events we had heard nothing of Herr von Blenheim, a fact from which I deduced with thankfulness that he was temporarily stunned. Unluckily, he now recovered. As I stood victorious, but breathless, my cap lost in the scuffle and my coat torn, I heard him stirring, and an instant later he pulled himself to his feet and flashed on an electric torch.

By its weird beam I saw that Miss Falconer was close beside me. Good heavens! Why, I though in anguish, wasn't she already upstairs? But I knew only too well; she wouldn't desert her champion. It was probably too late now. Blenheim, much congested as to countenance, seemed on the point of springing; his battered aids were struggling up in menacing, if unsteady, fashion; and Mr. Schwartzmann, at length provided with the light he wanted, was aiming at me with ominous deliberation from his coign of vantage above.

However, we were at the circular staircase. Again I caught up the table and held it before us as a shield while we climbed upward, side by side. In the distance my friend Schwartzmann was hopefully potting at us. A bullet, with a sharp ping, embedded itself in the thick wood in harmless fashion; another struck the shaft beside me, splintering its stone. We were at the last turn - but our pursuers were climbing also. I bent forward and let them have the table, hurling it with all possible force.

As it catapulted down upon them it knocked Blenheim off his balance, and he in his unforeseen descent swept the others from their feet. A swearing, groaning mass, a conglomeration of helplessly waving arms and legs, they rolled downward. Victory! I was about to join Miss Falconer in the doorway when there came a final flash from the opposite staircase, and I felt a stinging sensation across my forehead and a spurt of blood into my eyes.

The pain of the slight wound promptly altered my intentions. Instead of leaving the gallery, I sprang forward to the balustrade. Whipping my revolver out at last, I aimed deliberately and fired; whereupon I had the pleasure of seeing Mr. Schwartzmann rock, struggle, apparently regain his equilibrium, and then suddenly crumple up and pitch headlong down the stairs.

Below, Blenheim and his friend were extricating themselves from that blessed table. I passed through the door and thrust it shut and shot the bolts. We were safe for the present. I could not see Miss Falconer, nor did she speak to me; but her hand groped for my arm and rested there, and I covered it with one of mine.

Then, as we stood contentedly drawing breath, we heard steps mounting the staircase. Some one struck a vicious blow against the heavy door. Blenheim's voice, hoarse and muffled, reached us through the panels.

"Can you hear me there?" it asked.

If tones could kill! I summoned breath enough to answer with cheerful coolness.

"Every syllable," I responded. "What did you wish to say?"

"Just this." He was panting, either with exhaustion or fury, and there were slow, labored pauses between his words. "I will give you half an hour, exactly, to come out - with the papers. After that we will break the door down. And then you can say your prayers."

CHAPTER XXII

THE GUEST OF PREZELAY

The sanctuary into which we had stumbled was as black as Erebus save for one dimly grayish patch, which, I surmised, meant a window. When those heavy feet had clumped down the staircase, silence enveloped us again, beatific silence. Instantly I banished the late Mr. Van Blarcom from my consciousness. With a good stout door between us what importance had his threats?

The truth was that my blood was singing through my veins and my spirits were soaring. I would gladly have stood there forever, triumphant in the dark, with Miss Falconer's soft, warm fingers trembling a little, but lying in contented, almost cosy, fashion under mine. Had there ever been such a girl, at once so sweet and so daring? To think how she had waited for me all through that battle below!

A little breathless murmur came to me through the darkness.

"Oh, Mr. Bayne! You were so wonderful! How am I ever going to thank you?" was what it said.

"You needn't. Let me thank you for letting me in on it!" I exulted happily. "I give you my word, I haven't enjoyed anything so much in years. It was all a hallucination, of course; but it was jolly while it lasted. I was only worried every instant for fear the hall and the men would vanish, like an Arabian Nights' palace or the Great Horn Spoon or Aladdin's jinn!"

Very gently she withdrew her fingers, and my mood toppled ludicrously. Why had I been rejoicing? We were in the deuce of a mess! So far I had simply won a half hour's respite to be followed by the deluge; for if Blenheim had been ruthless before, what were his probable intentions now?

"We have lost our candle in the fracas," I muttered lamely.

"It doesn't matter. I have another," she answered in a soft, unsteady voice.

As she coaxed the light into being, I made a rapid survey. We were in a room of gray stone, of no great size and quite bare of furnishing, save for a few stone benches built into alcoves in the wall. The bareness of the scene emphasized our lack of resources. As a sole ray of hope, I perceived a possible line of retreat if things should grow too warm for us, a door facing the one by which we had come in.

With all the excitement, I had forgotten Mr. Schwartzmann's bullet, which, I have no doubt, had left me a gory spectacle. At any rate, I frightened Miss Falconer when the candle-light revealed me. In an instant she was bending over me, forcing me gently down upon a particularly cold, hard bench.

"They shot you!" she was exclaiming. Her voice was

low, but it held an astonishing protective fierceness. "They - they dared to hurt you! Oh, why didn't you tell me? Is it very bad?"

"No! no!" I protested, dabbing futilely at my forehead. "It isn't of the least importance. I assure you it is only a scratch. In fact," I groaned, "nobody could hurt my head; it is too solid. It must be ivory. If I had had a vestige of intelligence, an iota of it, the palest glimmer, I should have known from the beginning exactly who these fellows were!"

She was sitting beside me now, bending forward, all consoling eagerness.

"That is ridiculous!" she declared. "How could you guess?"

"Easily enough," I murmured. "I had all the clues at Gibraltar. Why, yesterday, on my way to your house in the rue St.-Dominique, I went over the whole case in the taxi, and still I didn't see. I let the fellow confide in me on the ship and warn me on the train and give me a final solemn ultimatum at the inn last night and come on here to frighten you and threaten you - when just a word to the police would have settled him forever. By George, I can't believe it! I should take a prize at an idiot show."

She laughed unsteadily.

"I don't see that," she answered. "Why should you have suspected him when even the authorities didn't guess? You are not a detective. You are a - a very brave, generous gentleman, who trusted a girl against all the evidence and helped her and protected her and risked your life for hers. Isn't that enough? And about their frightening me downstairs - they didn't. You see, Mr. Bayne - you were there."

A wisp of red-brown hair had come loose across her forehead. Her face, flushed and royally grateful, was smiling into mine. Till that moment I had never dreamed that eyes could be so dazzling. I thrust my hands deep into my pockets; I felt they were safer so.

"What is it?" she faltered, a little startled, as I rose.

"Nothing - now," I replied firmly. "I'll tell you later, to-morrow maybe, when we have seen this thing through. And in the meantime, whatever happens, I don't want you to give a thought to it. The German doesn't live who can get the better of me - not after what you have said."

The situation suddenly presented itself in rosy colors. I saw how strong the door was, what a lot of breaking it would take. And if they did force a way in, then I could try some sharp-shooting. But Miss Falconer was getting up slowly.

"Now the papers, Mr. Bayne," said she.

To be sure, the papers! I had temporarily forgotten them.

"They can't be here," I said blankly, gazing about the room.

"No, not here. In there." She motioned toward the inner door. "This is the old suite of the lords of Prezelay. We are in the room of the guards, where the armed retainers used to lie all night before the fire, watching. Then comes the antechamber and then the room of the squires and then the bedchamber of the lord." Her voice had fallen now as if she thought that the walls were listening. "In the lord's room there is a secret hiding-place behind a panel; and if the papers are at Prezelay, they will be there."

I took the candle from her, turned to the door, and opened it.

"I hope they are," I said. "Let us go and see."

The antechamber, the room of the squires, the bedchamber of the lord. Such terms were fascinating; they called up before me a whole picture of feudal life. Thanks to the attentions of the Germans, the rooms were mere empty shells, however, though they must have been rather splendid when decked out with furniture and portraits and tapestries before the war.

Our steps echoed on the stone as we traversed the antechamber, a quaint round place, lined with bull's-eye windows and presided over by the statues of four armed men. Another door gave us entrance to the quarter of the squires. We started across it, but in the center of the floor I stopped. In all the other rooms of the castle dust had lain thick, but there was none here. Elsewhere the windows had been closed and the air heavy and musty, but here the soft night breeze was drifting in. On a table, in odd conjunction, stood the remains of a meal, a roll of bandages, and a half-burned candle; and finally, against the wall lay a bed of a sort, a mattress piled with tumbled sheets.

Were these Marie-Jeanne's quarters? I did not know,

but I doubted. I turned to the girl.

"Miss Falconer," I said, attempting naturalness, "will you go back to the guard-room and wait there a few minutes, please? I think - that is, it seems just possible that some one is hiding in yonder. I'd prefer to investigate alone if you don't mind."

I broke off, suddenly aware of the look she was casting round her. It did not mean fear; it could mean nothing but an incredulous, dawning hope. These signs of occupancy suggested to her something so wonderful, so desirable that she simply dared not credit them; she was dreading that they might slip through her fingers and fade away! I made a valiant effort at understanding.

"Perhaps," I said, "you're expecting some one. Did you think that a - a friend of yours might have arrived here before we came?" She did not glance at me, but she bent her head, assenting. All her attention was focused raptly on that bed beside the wall.

"Yes," she whispered; "a long time before us. A month ago at least." Her eyes had begun to shine. "Oh, I don't dare to believe it; I've hardly dared to hope for it. But if it is true, I am going to be happier than I ever thought I could be again."

She made a swift movement toward the door, but I forestalled her. Whatever that room held, I must have a look at it before she went. I flung the door open, blocked her passage, and stopped in my tracks, for the best of reasons. A young man was sitting on a battered oak chest beneath a window, facing me, and in his right hand, propped on his knees, there glittered a

Marion Polk Angellotti

revolver that was pointed straight at my heart.

I stood petrified, measuring him. He was lightly built and slender. He had a manner as glittering as his weapon, and a pair of remarkably cool and clear gray eyes. His picturesqueness seemed wasted on mere flesh and blood it was so perfect. Coatless, but wearing a shirt of the finest linen, he looked like some old French duelist and ought, I felt, to be gazing at me, rapier in hand, from a gilt-framed canvas on the wall.

In the brief pause before he spoke I gathered some further data. He was a sick man and he had recently been wounded; at present he was keeping up by sheer courage, not by strength. His lips were pressed in a straight line, his eyes were shadowed, and his pallor was ghastly. Finally, he was wearing his left arm in a sling across his breast.

"Monsieur," he now enunciated clearly, "will raise both hands and keep them lifted. Monsieur sees, doubtless, that I am in no state for a wrestling-match. For that very reason he must take all pains not to forget himself - for should he stir, however slightly, I grieve to say that I must shoot."

The casualness of his tones made Blenheim's menaces seem childish and futile. I had not the slightest doubt that he would keep his word. Yet, without any reason whatever, I liked him and I had no fear of him; I did not feel for a single instant that Miss Falconer was in danger; she was as safe with him, I knew instinctively, as she was with me.

I opened my lips to parley, but found myself interrupted. A cry came from behind me, a low, utterly rapturous cry. I was thrust aside, and saw the girl spring past me. An instant later she was by the stranger, kneeling, with her arms about him and her bright head against his cheek.

"Jean! Dear Jean!" she was crying between tears and laughter. "We thought you were dead! We thought you were never coming back to Raincy-la-Tour!"

It seemed to me that some one had struck my head a stunning blow. For an interval I stood dazed; then, painfully, my brain stirred. Things went dancing across it like sharp, stabbing little flames, guesses, memories, scraps of talk I had heard, items I had read; but they were scattered, without cohesion; like will-o'-the-wisps, they could not be seized.

There was a young man, a noble of France, who had been a hero. I had read of him in a certain extra, as my steamer left New York. He had disappeared. Certain papers had vanished with him. He had been suspected, because it was known that the Germans wanted those special documents. All the world, I thought dully, seemed to be hunting papers; the French, the Germans, Miss Falconer, and I.

Once more I looked at the man on the chest. He had dropped his pistol and was clasping the girl to him, soothing her, stroking her hair. My brain began to work more rapidly. The little flashes of light seemed to run together, to crystallize into a whole. I knew.

Jean-Herve-Marie-Olivier, the Duke of Raincy-la-Tour, the Firefly of France.

CHAPTER XXIII

THE FIREFLY OF FRANCE

He was very weak indeed; it seemed a miracle that, at the sounds below, he had found strength to drag himself from his bed and crawl inch by inch to the room of the secret panel to mount guard there; and no sooner had he soothed Miss Falconer than he collapsed in a sort of swoon. We laid him on the chest, and I fetched a pillow for his head and stripped off my coat and spread it over him. I took out my pocket-flask, too, and forced a few drops between his teeth. In short I tried to play the game.

When his eyes opened, however, my endurance had reached its limits. With a muttered excuse, - not that I flattered myself they wanted me to stay! - I left them and stumbled into the room of the squires, taking refuge in the grateful dark. I don't know how long I sat there, elbows on knees, hands propping my head; but it was a ghastly vigil. In this round, unlike the battle in the hall, I had not been victor. Instead, I had taken the count.

I knew now, of course, that I was in love with Esme Falconer. Judging from the violence of the sensation, I must have loved her for quite a while. Probably it had begun that night in the St. Ives restaurant; for when before had I watched any girl with such special, ecstatic, almost proprietary rapture? Yes, that was why, ever since, I had been cutting such crazy capers. From first to last they were the natural thing, the prerogative of a man in my state of mind or heart.

Many threads of the affair still remained to be unraveled. I didn't know what the duke was doing here, what he had been about for a month past, how the girl, far off in America, had guessed his whereabouts and his need; nor did I care. His mere existence was enough - that and Esme's love for him. All my interest in my Chinese puzzle had come to a wretched end.

"Confound him!" I thought savagely. "We could have spared him perfectly. What business has he turning up at the eleventh hour? He didn't cross the ocean with her. He didn't suspect her unforgivably. He didn't help her, and disguise himself as a chauffeur for her, and wing Schwartzmann, and bruise up the other chaps and send them rolling in a heap. This is my adventure. He must have had a hundred. Why couldn't he stick to his high-flying and dazzling and let me alone?"

The murmur of voices drifted from the lord's bedchamber. I could guess what they had to say to each other, Miss Falconer and her duke. The Firefly of France! Even I, a benighted foreigner, knew the things that title stood for: heroism, in a land where every soldier was a hero; praise and medals and glory; thirty conquered aeroplanes - a record over which his ancestors, those old marshals and constables lying effigied on their tombs of marble with their feet resting on carved lions, must nod their heads with pride.

"Mr. Bayne!"

It was Miss Falconer's voice. I rose reluctantly and obeyed the summons. The Firefly was sitting propped on the chest, white, but steadier, while Esme still knelt beside him, holding his hand in hers.

"I have been telling Jean, Mr. Bayne, how you have helped us." The radiance of her face, the lilt of her voice, stabbed me with a jealous pang. I wanted to see her happy, Heaven knew, but not quite in this manner. "And he wants to thank you for all that you have done."

The Duke of Raincy-la-Tour spoke to me in English that was correct, but quaintly formal, of a decided charm.

"Monsieur," he said, "I offer you my gratitude. And if you will touch the hand of one concerning whom, I fear, very evil things are believed -"

I forced a smile and a hearty pressure.

"I'll risk it," I assured him. "The chain of evidence against you seemed far-fetched to say the least. They pointed out accusingly that your father and your grand-father had been royalists, and that therefore -"

He made a gesture.

"May their souls find repose! Monsieur, it is true that they were. But if they lived to-day, my father and grandfather, they would not be traitors. They would wear, like me, the uniform of France."

He smiled, and I knew once for all that I could never hate him; that mere envy and a shame of it were the worst that I could feel. Everything about him won me, his simplicity, his fine pride, his clearness of eye and voice, his look of a swift, polished sword blade. I had never seen a man like him. The Duchess of Raincy-la-Tour would be a lucky woman; so much was plain.

I found a seat on the window ledge, the girl remained kneeling by him, and he told us his story, always in that quaint, formal speech. As it went on it absorbed me. I even forgot those clasped hands for an occasional instant. In every detail, in every quiet sentence, there was some note that brought before me the Firefly's achievements, the marauding airships he had climbed into the air to meet, the foes he had swooped from the blue to conquer, his darts into the land of his enemies where there was a price upon his head.

The story had to do with a night when he had left the French lines behind him. His commander had been quite frank. The mission meant his probable death. He was to wear a German uniform; to land inside the lines of the kaiser, to conceal his plane, if luck favored him, among the trees in the grounds of the old chateau of Ranceville; to get what knowledge and sketch what plans he could of defenses against which the French attacks had hitherto broken vainly, and to bring them home.

All had gone well at first. His gallant little plane had winged its way into the unknown like a darting swallow; he had landed safely; and after he had walked for hours with the Germans about him and death beside him, he had gained his spoils. It was as he rose for the return flight that the alarm was given. He got away; but he had five hostile aircraft after him. Could he hope to elude them and to land safely at the French lines?

It was in that hour, while the night lingered and the stars still shone and the cannon of the two armies challenged each other steadily, that the Firefly of France fought his greatest battle in the air. Since his whole aim was escape, it was bloodless; he had to trust to skill and cunning; he dared manoeuvers that appalled others, dropped plummet-like, looped dizzily, soared to the sheerest heights. He had been wounded. The framework of his plane was damaged. Still he gained on his foes and won through to the lines of France.

"But I might not land there," he explained. "The Germans followed. A mist had closed about us, hiding us from my friends below. I heard only my propeller; and that, by now, sounded faint to me, for I was weakening; one shot had hit my shoulder and another had wounded my left arm."

The girl swayed closer against him, watching him with eyes of worship. Well, I didn't wonder, though it cut me to the heart. Even a fairy prince could have been no worthier of her than this Jean-Herve-Marie-Olivier; of that at least, I told myself dourly, I must be glad.

"As I raced on," said the duke, "there came a certain thought to me. We had traveled far; we were in the country near Prezelay, my cousin's house. The village, I knew, was ruined, but the chateau stood; and if I could reach it, old Marie-Jeanne would help me. You comprehend, my weakness was growing. I knew I had little more time."

The shrouding mist had aided him to lose those pursuing vultures. The last of them fell off, baffled, - or afraid to go deeper into France. Now he emerged again into the clear air and the starlight. The land beneath him was a scudding blur, with a dark-green mass in its center, the forest of La Fay.

And then, suddenly, he knew he must land if he were not to lose consciousness and hurtle down blindly; and with set teeth and sweat beading his forehead, he began the descent. At the end his strength failed him. The plane crashed among the trees. "But Saint Denis, who helps all Frenchmen, helped me," - he smiled - "and I was thrown clear."

From that thicket where his machine lay hidden it was a mile to Prezelay. He dragged himself over this distance, sometimes on his hands and knees. Soon after dawn Marie-Jeanne, answering a discordant ringing, found a man lying outside the gate and babbling deliriously, her master's cousin, in a blood-soaked uniform, holding out a bundle of papers, and begging her by the soul of her mother to put them in the castle's secret hiding-place.

She did it. Then she coaxed the wounded man to the rooms opening from the gallery and tended him day and night through the weeks of fever that ensued. From his ravings she learned that he was in danger and feared pursuers; and with the peasant's instinct for caution, she had not dared to send for help.

"It was yesterday," the duke told us, "that my mind came back. I knew then what must be thought of me, what must be said of me, all over France." He was leaning on the wall now, exhausted and white, but dauntless. "No matter for that - I have the papers. You recall the hiding-place?"

He smiled as he asked the question, and Miss Falconer smiled back at him. Getting to her feet, she ran her fingers across the oak panel over his head, where for centuries a huntsman had been riding across a forest glade and blowing his horn. The bundle of his hunting-knife protruded just a little; and as the girl pressed it, the panel glided silently open, revealing a space, square and dark and cobwebby.

Something was lying there, a thin, wafer-like packet of papers, the papers for which the Firefly of France had shed his blood. She held them up in triumph. But the duke was still smiling faintly. He thrust one hand into his shirt and drew out a duplicate package, which he raised for us to see.

"Behold!" he said. "They are copies. All that I sketched that night near Ranceville, all that I wrote - I did not once, but twice. These I carried openly, to be found if I were captured. But those you hold went hidden in the sole of my boot, which was hollowed for them, so that if I were taken and then escaped, they might go too!"

I had read of such devices, I remembered vaguely. There was a story of a young French captain who had tried the trick in Champagne and succeeded with it, a rather famous exploit. Then I thought of something else. I got up slowly.

"You have two sets of papers?" I repeated.

"As you see, Monsieur."

"Then I'll take one of them," said I.

Miss Falconer was looking at me in a puzzled fashion.

As for the duke, his brows drew together; his figure straightened; the cool glint grew in his eyes.

"Monsieur," he stated somewhat icily, "such things as these are not souvenirs. When they leave my possession they will go to the supreme command."

"Certainly," I agreed, unruffled. "That will do admirably for the first package; but about the second - no doubt Miss Falconer told you that we have German guests downstairs? Perhaps she forgot to mention the leader's name, though. It is Franz von Blenheim. And I don't care to have him break down the door and burst in on us, on her specially; I would rather, all things considered, interview him in the hall."

The Firefly's face had altered at the name of the secret agent; he was now regarding me with intentness, but without a frown. As for Miss Falconer, the trouble in her eyes was growing. I should have to be careful. Accordingly I summoned a debonair manner as I went on.

"If you'll allow me," I said, "I will take the papers down to him. He won't know that they are copies; he will snatch at them, glad of the chance. And since he is in a hurry, he probably won't stop to parley. He will simply be off at top speed, and leave us safe.

"Of course, that is the one unpleasant feature of the affair, his going." At this point I glanced in a casual manner at the Duke of Raincy-la-Tour. "It seems a pity to let him walk off scot-free, to plan more trouble for France; but that is past praying for. I could hardly hope to stop him, except by a miracle. If there is one, I'll be on hand."

Marion Polk Angellotti

Would the duke guess the hope with which I was going downstairs, I wondered. I thought he did, for his eyes flashed slightly, and he stirred a little on the chest.

"Such a miracle, Monsieur," he remarked, "would serve France greatly. As a good son of the Church, I will pray for it with all my heart!"

"I hope to come back," I went on, "and rejoin you. But if I shouldn't for any reason," - with careful vagueness, - "you must stay here, barricaded, till they are gone. Then Miss Falconer can drive her car to the nearest town and bring back help for you. You see, it will be entirely simple, either way."

The girl, very white now, took a swift step toward me.

"Simple?" she cried. "They will kill you! They hate you, Mr. Bayne, and they are four to one. You mustn't go."

But the duke's hand was on her arm.

"My dear," he said, "he has reason. This friend of yours, I perceive, is a gallant gentleman. Believe me, if I had strength to stand, he would not go alone."

He held out the papers to me, and I took them. Then we clasped hands, the Firefly and I.

"*Bonne chance, Monsieur,*" he bade me with the pressure.

"Good luck and good-bye," I answered. "Miss Falconer, will you come to the door?"

She took up the candle and came forward to light me, and we went in silence through the room of the squires and through the ante-chamber and into the room of the guards. She walked close beside me; her eyes shone wet; her lips trembled. There were things I would have given the world to say, but I suppressed them. To the very end, I had resolved, I would play fair. We were at the outer door.

"Good-by, Miss Falconer," I said, halting. "You mustn't worry; everything is going to turn out splendidly, I am sure. Only, now that we have the papers, it ends our little adventure, doesn't it? So before I go I want to thank you for our day together. It has been wonderful. There never was another like it. I shall always be thankful for it, no matter what I have to pay."

I stopped abruptly, realizing that this was not cricket. To make up, I put out my hand quite coolly; but she grasped it in both of hers and held it in a soft, warm clasp.

"I shall never forget," she whispered. "Come back to us, Mr. Bayne!"

For a moment I looked at her in the light of the candle, at her lovely face, at the ruddy hair framing it, at the tears heavy on her lashes. Then I drew the bolt and went out and heard her fasten the door.

CHAPTER XXIV

THE OBUS

I stood in the gallery for an instant, indulging in a reconnoissance. The hall was now illuminated by an electric torch and three guttering candles; at the foot of the staircase lay the table which had done such yeoman's service, split in two. As for the besiegers, they were gathered near the chimney-place in a worse-for-wear group, one nursing a nosebleed; another feeling gingerly of a loose tooth; Blenheim himself frankly raging, and decorated with a broad cut across his forehead and a cheek that was rapidly taking on assorted shades of blue, green, and black; and the redoubtable Mr. Schwartzmann, worst off of all, lying in a heap, groaning at intervals, but apparently quite unaware of what was going on.

My abrupt sally seemed transfixing. I might have been Medusa. I had a welcome minute in which to contemplate the victims of my prowess and to exult unchristianly in their scars. Then the tableau dissolved, the three men sprang up, and I took action. As I emerged I had drawn out a handkerchief and I now proceeded to raise and wave it.

"Well, Herr von Blenheim, I have come to parley with you," I announced, "white flag and all."

He tried to look as if he had expected me, though it was obvious that he hadn't. To give verisimilitude to the pretense, he even pulled out his watch.

"I thought you would. You had just two minutes' grace," he commented, watching me narrowly. "Suppose you come down. You have brought the papers, I hope - for your own sake?"

"Oh, yes!" I assured him with all possible blandness. "I have brought them. What else was there to do? You had us in the palm of your hand. That door is old and worm-eaten; you could have crumpled it up like paper. When we thought the situation over we saw its hopelessness at once; so here I am."

"That is sensible," he agreed curtly, though I could see that he was puzzled. Casting a baffled glance beyond me, he scanned the gallery door. It by no means merited my description, being heavy, solid, almost immovable in aspect. "Well, let's have the papers!" he said, with suspicion in his tone.

I descended in a deliberate manner, casting alert eyes about me, for, to use an expressive idiom, I was not doing this for my health. On the contrary I had two very definite purposes; the first, which I could probably compass, was to save Miss Falconer from further intercourse with Blenheim and to conceal the presence of the wounded, helpless Firefly from his enemies; the second, surprisingly modest, was to make the four Germans prisoners and hand them over in triumph to the gendarmes of the nearest town, Santierre.

I was perfectly aware of the absurdity of this ambition.

I lacked the ghost of an idea of how to set about the thing. But the general craziness of events had unhinged me. I was forming the habit of trusting to pure luck and *vogue la galere*! I can't swear that I hadn't visions of conquering all my adversaries in some miraculous single-handed fashion, disarming them, and, as a final sweet touch of revenge, tying them up in chairs, to keep Marie-Jeanne company and meditate on the turns of fate.

"Here they are," I said, obligingly offering the package. "We found them nestling behind a panel - old family hiding place, you know. I can't vouch for their contents, not being an expert, but Miss Falconer was satisfied. How about it, now you look at them? Do they seem all right?"

Not paying the slightest attention to my conversational efforts, Blenheim had snatched the papers, torn them hungrily open, and run them through. He was bristling with suspicion; but he evidently knew his business. It did not take him long to conclude that he really had his spoils.

Folding them up carefully, he thrust them into his coat and stored them, displaying, however, less triumph than I had thought he would. The truth was that he looked preoccupied, and I wondered why. For the first time in all the hair-trigger situations that I had seen him face I sensed a strain in him.

"So much for that. Now, Mr. Bayne, what do you think we mean to do to you?" he asked.

"I don't know, I am sure," I answered rather absently; I was weighing the relative merits of jiu-jitsu and my five remaining revolver-shots. "Is there anything sufficiently lingering? Let me suggest boiling oil; or I understand that roasting over a slow fire is considered tasty. Either of those methods would appeal to you, wouldn't it?"

"I don't deny it!" Blenheim answered in a tone that was convincing. "You haven't endeared yourself to us, my friend, in the last hour. But we can't spare you yet; our plans for the evening are lively ones and they include you. I told you, didn't I, that we were going to no man's-land via the trenches, when we finished this affair?"

"You told me many interesting things. I've forgotten some of the details." I was aware of a thrill of excitement. The man was worried; so much was sure.

"You will recall them presently, or if you don't, I'll refresh your memory. The fact is, Mr. Bayne, you have put a pretty spoke in our wheel. It stands this way: our papers are made out for a party of four officers, and you have eliminated Schwartzmann. Don't you owe us some amends for that? You like disguises, I gather from your costume. What do you say to putting on a new one, a pale-blue uniform, and seeing us through the lines?"

He looked, while uttering this wild pleasantry, about as humorous as King Attila. Could he possibly be in earnest? After all, perhaps he was! War rules were cast-iron things; if his pass called for four men, four he must have or rouse suspicion; and it was certain that Herr Schwartzmann would do no gadding to-night or for many nights to come. That shot of mine from the gallery had upset Blenheim's plans very neatly. I stared at him, fascinated.

"Well?" said he. "Do you understand?"

"I understand," I exclaimed indignantly, "that this is too much! It is, really. I was getting hardened; I could stand a mere impossibility or two and not blink; but this! It is beyond the bounds. I shall begin to see green snakes presently or writhing sea-serpents -"

"No," Blenheim cut me short savagely, "you are underestimating. Unless you oblige us what you will see is the hereafter, Mr. Bayne!"

Yes, he meant it. His very fierceness, eloquent of frazzled nerves, was proof conclusive. With another thrill, triumphant this time, I recognized my chance. His campaign, instead of going according to specifications, had been interfered with; his position was dangerous; he had no time to lose; for all he knew, at any point along the road his masquerade might have been suspected, the authorities notified, vengeance put on his track. In desperation he meant to risk my denouncing him, use me till he reached the Front trenches and his friends there, and then, no doubt, get rid of me. What he couldn't guess was that I would have turned the earth upside down to make this opportunity that he was offering me on a silver tray.

"Oh, I'll oblige you," I assured him with what must have seemed insane cheerfulness. "I'll oblige you, Her von Blenheim, with all the pleasure in the world. If you really want me, that is. If my presence won't make you nervous. Aren't you afraid, for instance, that I might be tempted to share my knowledge of your name and your profession with the first French soldiers we meet?"

"As to that, we will take our chances." Blenheim's face was adamant, though my suggestion had produced a not entirely enlivening effect on his two friends. "You see, Mr. Bayne, in this business the risks will be mostly yours. There will be no flights of stairs to dart up and no tables to over turn and no candles to extinguish; you will sit in the tonneau with a man beside you, a very watchful man, and a pistol against your side. You don't want to die, do you? I thought not, since you surrendered those papers. Well, then, you'll be wise not to say a word or stir a muscle. And now we are in a hurry. Will you make your toilet, please?"

It was the bizarre curtain scene of what I had called an extravaganza. Blenheim's confederates, taking no special pains for gentleness, stripped off the outer garments of the prostrate Schwartzmann, who moaned and groaned throughout the process, though he never opened his eyes. Blenheim urged haste upon us; he was getting more fidgety every instant; he bit his lip, drummed with his fingers, kept an ear cocked, as if expecting to hear pursuers at the door. Still, he neglected no precautions. He demanded my revolver. I surrendered it amiably, and then doffed my chauffeur's outfit and took, from a social standpoint, a gratifying step upward, donning one by one the insignia of France.

The fit was not perfect by any means. Schwartzmann was a giant, a mountain. My feet swished aloud groggily in his burnished putties; his garments hung round me in ample, rather than graceful, folds. However, the loose cape of horizon blue resembled charity in covering defects. As a dummy, sitting

Marion Polk Angellotti

motionless in the rear of the automobile, my captors felt that I would pass.

By this time I was enchanted with the plans I was concocting. I might look like an opera-bouffe hero, - no doubt I did, - but my hour would come. Meanwhile events were marching. My transformation being complete, Blenheim gave a curt order in German, the candles were blown out, and lighted only by the torch, we turned toward the door. There was an inarticulate cry from Schwartzmann, just conscious enough, poor beggar, to grasp the fact of his abandonment in the strategic retreat his friends were beating. Then we were out in the courtyard, beneath the stars.

Down the hill, sheltered behind the stones of a ruined house, the gray car was waiting, and Blenheim climbed into the driver's seat, meanwhile giving brief directions. There was no noise, no flurry; the affair, I must say, went with an efficiency in keeping with the proudest Prussian traditions. I was installed in the tonneau, and I was hardly seated before the motor hummed into life, and we jolted into the moonlit road.

For perhaps the hundredth time I asked myself if I was dreaming; if this person in a French disguise, speeding through the night with a blue-clad German beside him, - a German suffering, by the way, from a headache, the last stages of a nosebleed, and a pronounced dislike for me as the agency responsible for his ailments, - was really Devereux Bayne. But the air was cold on my face; a revolver pressed my side; I saw three set, hard profiles. It was not a dream; it was a dash for safety. And it was engineered by anxious, desperate men.

Blenheim, hunched over the steering wheel, had settled to his business. Certainly his nerve was going; the mania for escape had caught him; he took startling chances on his curves and turns. Still, he knew the country, it seemed. We drove on, fast and furiously, by lanes, by mere paths set among thickets, by narrow brushwood roads. Sometimes we skirted the river, which shone silver in the moonlight, lined with rushes. Again, we could see nothing but a roof of trees overhead.

We emerged into a wider road, and I became award of various noises; a booming, clear and regular; the sound of voices; the rumbling of many wheels. We must be nearing the Front; we were rejoining the main highroad. My guess was proved correct at the next turning, where a sentry barred our path.

The sight of his honest French face was like a tonic to me. In some welcome way it seemed to hearten me for my task. The pistol of my friend in the tonneau bored through his cape into my side; I sat very quiet. If I did this four, five, perhaps six times, they might think me cowed and relax their vigilance. Their suspicions would be lulled by my tractability and their contempt. Then my hour would strike.

Satisfied with the safe-conducts, the sentry gestured us forward, and his figure slipped out of my vision as the gray car purred on. The man beside me chuckled.

"Behold this Yankee! He is as good as gold, my captain. He sits like a mouse," he announced in his own tongue.

"He'll be wise," Blenheim announced, "to go on doing

so." The threat was in English for my benefit and came from between his teeth.

In front of us the noise was growing. With our next turn we entered the highroad, taking our place in a long rumbling line of ambulances and supply-carts and laboring camions, or trucks. We glimpsed faces, heard voices all about us. The change from solitude to this unbroken procession was bewildering. But we did not long remain a part of it; we turned again into narrower lanes.

The control was growing stricter. Four separate times we were halted, and always I sat hunched in my corner as impassive as a stone. The more deeply we penetrated toward the Front, the more uneasy grew my companions. Each time that a sentry halted us they waited in more anxiety for his verdict. The man beside me, it was true, still menaced me with his pistol point; but the gesture had grown perfunctory. He did not think I would attempt anything. He believed now that I was afraid.

Our road crossed a hilltop, and I saw beneath us a valley, streaked at intervals with blinding signal-flashes of red and green. In my ears the thunder of the guns was growing steadily. When we were stopped again, the sentry warned us. The road we were traveling, he said, had been intermittently under fire for two days.

It looked, indeed, as if devils had used it for a playground; the trees were mere blackened stumps; the fields on each side stretched burnt and bare. And then came the climax: something passed us, - high above our heads, I fancy, though its frightful winds seemed brushing us, - a ghost of the night, an aerial demon, a shrieking thing that made the man beside me cringe and shudder. It was new to me, but I could not mistake it. It was what the French call an *obus*, a word that in some subtle manner seems more menacing and dreadful than our own term of shell.

As we sped on I leaned against the cushions, outwardly quiet. Inwardly, I was gathering myself together for my attempt. I had not thought I would first approach the Front this way; but it was a good way, I had a good object. At the next stop, whatever it was, I meant to make the venture. I did not doubt I should succeed in it. But I could not hope to keep my life.

Another *obus* hurtled over us and shrieked away into the distance; and again the man beside me flinched, but I did not. I was thinking, with odd lucidity, of many things, among them Dunny and his old house in Washington, into which I should never again let myself with my latch-key, sure of a welcome at any hour of the day or night. My guardian's gray head rose before me. My heart tightened. The finest, straightest old chap who ever took a forlorn little tike in out of the wet, and petted him, and frolicked with him, and filled his stocking all the year round, and made his holidays things of rapture, and taught him how to ride and shoot and fish and swim and cut his losses and do pretty much everything that makes life worth living - that was Dunny.

"This will be a hard jolt for the old chap," I thought, "but he'll say that I played the game."

And Esme Falconer, my own brave, lovely Esme! "She has come down the staircase now," I told myself. "She has untied Marie-Jeanne. She has gone out and started the car." What would she think of my disappearance? Well, she wouldn't misjudge me, I felt sure; and neither would Jean-Herve-Marie-Olivier. He would know that I was acting as, in my place, he would have acted, that I didn't mean to let Franz von Blenheim defy France and go off untouched.

The whole world seemed mysteriously to have narrowed to one girl, Esme. How I had lived before I saw her; how, having seen her, I could ever have lived without her, - I didn't know. But the sound of grinding brakes roused me. We were slowing up in obedience to a signal from a canvas-covered, half-demolished shelter filled with men in blue uniforms; we were coming to a standstill. Blenheim leaned out, and for a moment I saw his face in the beam of light from the sentry's lantern. It looked thin and set. He was giving beneath the strain.

"Behold my comrade!" He thrust our papers into the hands of the sentry. "And make haste, for the love of heaven! We are waited for *la-bas*."

I cast a quick glance at my body-guard, whose anxious eyes were on the sentinel. His pistol still lay against my side, but his thoughts were far away. It was the moment. With the rapidity of lightning I knocked his arm up, caught his wrist, and clung to it, calling out simultaneously in a voice of crisp command.

"My friends," I cried in French, "I order you to arrest these persons! They are agents of the kaiser! They are German spies!"

The pistol, clutched between us, exploded harmlessly

into the air. I head shouts, saw men running toward us. Then I caught sight of Blenheim's face, dark and oddly contorted; he had turned and was leveling his revolver at me, resting one knee on the driver's seat as he took deliberate aim.

"I say," I cried again, struggling for the weapon, "that this is Franz von Blenheim, that these are men of the kaiser, spying, in disguise -"

It seemed to me that some one caught Blenheim's arm from behind just as he fired; but I was not certain. For suddenly that same whistling shriek sounded over us, nearer this time, more ominous; the earth seemed to rock and then to end in a mighty shock and cataclysm. Blackness enveloped me, and I dropped into a bottomless pit.

CHAPTER XXV

AT RAINCY-LA-TOUR

When I opened my eyes it was with a peculiarly reluctant feeling, for my eyelids were so heavy that they seemed to weigh a ton. My head was unspeakably groggy, and I had quite lost my memory. I couldn't, if suddenly interrogated, have replied with one intelligent bit of information about myself, not even with my name.

Flat on my back I was lying, gazing up at what, surprisingly, seemed to be a ceiling festooned with garlands of roses and painted with ladies and cavaliers, idling about a stretch of greensward, decidedly in the Watteau style. Where was I? What had happened to make me feel so helpless? It reminded me of an episode of my childhood, a day when my pony had fallen and rolled upon me, and I had been carried home with two crushed ribs and a broken arm.

Coming out at that time from the influence of the ether, I had found Dunny at my bedside. If only he were here now! I looked round. Why, there he was, sitting in a brocaded chair by the window, his dear old silver head thrown back, dozing beyond a doubt.

To see him gave me a warm, comforted, homelike

feeling. Nor did it surprise me, but my surroundings did. The room, a veritable Louis Quinze jewel in its paneling, carving, and gilding, might have come direct from Versailles by parcel post; my bed was garlanded and curtained in rose-color. Where I had gone to sleep last night I couldn't remember; but it hadn't, I was obstinately sure, been here.

What ailed me, anyhow? I began a series of cautious experiments, designed to discover the trouble. My arms were weak and of a strange, flabby limpness, but they moved. So did my left leg; but when I came to the right one I was baffled. It wouldn't stir; it was heavily encased in something. Good heavens! now I knew! It was in a plaster cast.

The shock of the discovery taught me something further, namely, that my head was liable to excruciating little throbs of pain. I raised a hand to it. My forehead was swathed in bandages, like a turbaned Turk's. Oh, to be sure, in the castle at Prezelay, as we were retreating up the staircase, Schwartzmann had fired at me; but, then, hadn't that been a pin prick, the merest scratch?

The name Prezelay served as a key to solve the puzzle. The whole fantastic, incredible chain of happenings came back to me in a rush; the gray car, the inn, the murder, the night in the castle, Jean-Herve-Marie-Olivier.

"Dunny!" I heard myself quavering in a voice utterly unlike my own.

The figure in the chair started up and hurried toward me, and then Dunny's hands were holding my hands, his eyes looking into mine.

"There, Dev, there! Take it easy," the familiar voice was soothing me. "Hold on to me, my boy, You are safe now. You're all right!"

My safety, however, seemed of small importance for the time being.

"Dunny," I implored, "listen! You have got to find out for me about a girl. How am I to tell you, though? If I start the story, you'll think I'm raving."

"I know all about it, Dev," my guardian reassured me. "I've seen Miss Falconer. She's absolutely safe."

If that were so, I could relax, and I did with fervent thankfulness. Not for long, however; my brain had begun to work.

"See here! I want to know who has been playing football with me," was my next demand, which Dunny answered obligingly, if with a slightly dubious face.

"That French doctor, nice young chap, said you weren't to talk," he muttered, "but if I were in your place I'd want to know a few things myself. It was this way, Dev. A fragment of a shell struck you -"

"A fragment!" I raised weak eyebrows. "I know better. Twenty shells at least, and whole!"

"- and didn't strike your Teuton friends," he charged on, suddenly purple of visage. "It was a true German shell, my boy, the devil looking after his own. The man in the seat with you was cut up a bit; the other two were thrown clear of the motor. If you hadn't already given the alarm, they would probably have got off scot-free. As it was, the French held a drumhead court martial a little later, and all three of the fellows - well, you can fill in the rest."

I was silent for a minute while a picture rose before me: a dank, gray dawn; a firing-squad, and Franz von Blenheim's dark, grim face. No doubt he had died bravely; but I could not pity him; I had too clear a recollection of the hall at Prezelay.

"As for you," Dunny was continuing, "you seem to have puzzled them finely. There you were in a French uniform, at your last gasp apparently, and with an American passport, that you seem to have clung to through thick and thin, inside your coat. They took a chance on you, though, because you had made them a present of the Franz von Blenheim; and by the next day, thanks to Miss Falconer and the Duke of Raincy-la-Tour, you were being looked for all over France.

"So that's how it stands. You're at Raincy-la-Tour now, at the duke's chateau. The place has been a hospital ever since the war began. Only you're not with the other wounded. You are - well - a rather special patient in the pavilion across the lake; and you're by way of being a hero. The day I landed, the first paper I saw shrieked at me how you had tracked the kaiser's star agent and outwitted him and handed him over to justice."

"The deuce it did!" I exclaimed. "You must have been puffed up with pride."

My guardian's jaw set itself rigidly. "I was too busy,"

was his grim answer. "You see, the end of the statement said there was no hope that you could survive. And when I got here I found you with fever, delirium, one leg shot up, four bits of shell in your head, a fine case of brain concussion. That was nearly three weeks ago, and it seems more like three years!"

An idea, at this point, made me fix a searching gaze on him.

"By the way," I asked accusingly, "how did you happen to arrive so opportunely on this side? It seemed as natural as possible to find you settled here waiting for my eyes to open; but on second thoughts I suppose you didn't fly?"

He looked extraordinarily embarrassed.

"Why," he growled at length, "I had business. I got a cablegram soon after you left New York. The thing was confoundedly inconvenient, but I had no choice about it."

"Dunny," I said weakly, but sternly, "you didn't bring me up to tell whoppers, not bare-faced ones like that, anyhow, that wouldn't deceive the veriest child. What earthly business could you have over here in war-time? Own up, now, and take your medicine like a man."

His guilty air was sufficient answer.

"Well, Dev," he acknowledged, "it was your cable. That Gibraltar mess was a nasty one, and I didn't like its looks. I'm getting old, and you're all I've got; so I took a passport and caught the *Rochambeau*. Not, of course, that I doubted your ability to take care of yourself, my boy -"

"Didn't you? You might have," I admitted with some ruefulness, "if you had known I was bucking both the Allied governments and the picked talent of the Central powers. It was too much. I was riding for a fall, and I got it. But I don't mind saying, Dunny, I'm infernally glad you came."

He wiped his eyes.

"Well, you go to sleep now," he counseled gruffly. "You've got to get well in a hurry; there's work for you to do! All sorts of things have been happening since that *obus* knocked you out. Just a week ago, for instance, the President went before Congress and -"

"What's that you say? Not war?"

"Yes, war, young man! We're in it at last, up to our necks; in it with men and ships and munitions and foodstuffs and everything else we have to help with, praise the Lord! You'll fight beneath the Stars and Stripes, instead of under the Tricolor. I say, Dev, that's positively the last word I'll utter. You've got to rest!"

In a weak, quavering fashion, but with sincere enthusiasm, I tried to celebrate by singing a few bars of the "Star-Spangled Banner" and a little of the "Marseillaise." Dunny was right, however; the conversation had exhausted me. In the midst of my patriotic demonstration I fell asleep.

My convalescence was a marvel, I learned from young Dr. Raimbault, the surgeon from the chateau who came to see me every day. According to him, I was a patient in a hundred, in a thousand; he never wearied of admiring my constitution, which he described by the various French equivalents of "as hard as nails." Not a set-back attended the course of my recovery. First, I sat propped up in bed; then I attained the dignity of an arm-chair; later, slowly and painfully, I began to drag myself about the room. But the day on which my physician's rapture burst all bounds was the great one when I crawled from the pavilion, gained a bench beneath the trees, and sat enthroned, glaring at my crutches. They were detestable implements; I longed to smash them. And they would, the doctor airily informed me, be my portion for three months.

To feel grumpy in such surroundings was certainly black ingratitude. It was an idyllic place. My pavilion was a sort of Trianon, a Marie Antoinette bower, all flowers and gold. Fresh green woods grew about it; a lake stretched before it; swans dotted the water where trees were mirrored, and there were marble steps and balustrades. Across this glittering expanse rose Raincy-la-Tour, proud and stately, with its formal gardens and its fountains and its Versailles-like front. In the afternoons I could see the wounded soldiers walking there or being pushed to and fro in wheel-chairs; legless and armless, some of them; wreckage of the mighty battle-fields; timely reminders, poor heroic fellows, that there were people in the world a great deal worse off than I.

Yet, instead of being thankful, I was profoundly wretched. I moped and sulked; I fell each day into a deeper, more consistent gloom. I tried grimly to regain my strength, with a view to seeking other quarters. While I stayed here I was the guest of the Firefly of France; and though I admired him, - I should have been a cad, a quitter, a poor loser, everything I had ever held anathema in days gone by, not to do so, - still I couldn't feel toward him as a man should feel toward his host; not in the least!

On three separate occasions Dunny motored up to Paris, bringing back as the fruits of his first excursion my baggage from the Ritz. I was clothed again, in my right mind; except for my swathed head, I looked highly civilized. The day when I had raced hither and yon, and fought an unbelievable battle in a dark hall, and insanely masqueraded first in a leather coat, then in a pale-blue uniform, seemed dim and far-off indeed.

"It was a nice hashish dream," I told my mirrored image. "But it wasn't real, my lad, for a moment; such things don't happen to folks like you. You're not the romantic type; you don't look like some one in an old picture; you haven't brought down thirty German aeroplanes or thereabouts, and won every war medal the French can give and the name of Ace. No; you look like a - a correct bulldog; and winning an occasional polo cup is about your limit. Even if it hadn't been settled before you met her, you wouldn't have stood a chance."

There were times when I prayed never to see Esme Falconer again. There were other times when I knew I would drag myself round the world - yes, on my crutches! - if at the end of the journey I could see her for an instant, a long way off. I could see that my despondency was driving Dunny to distraction. He evolved the theory that I was going into a decline.

Then came the afternoon that made history. I was sitting at my window. The trees seemed specially green, the sky specially blue, the lake specially bright. I was feeling stronger and was glumly planning a move to Paris when I saw an automobile speed up the poplared walk toward Raincy-la-Tour.

Rip-snorting and chugging, the thing executed a curve before the chateau, and then, hugging the side of the lake, advanced, obviously toward my humble abode. My heart seemed to turn a somersault. I should have known that car if I had met it in Bagdad. It was a long blue motor, polished to the last notch, deeply cushioned, luxurious, poignantly familiar, the car, in short, that I had pursued to Bleau, and that later, in flat defiance of President Poincare or the Generalissimo of France, or whoever makes army rules and regulations, I had guided through the war zone to the castle of Prezelay.

As the chauffeur halted it near the pavilion, it disgorged three occupants, one of who, a young officer, slender of form and gracefully alert of movement, wore the dark-blue uniform of the French Flying Corps. I knew him only too well. It was Jean-Herve-Marie-Olivier. But the glance I gave him was most cursory; my attention was focused hungrily on the two ladies in the tonneau. They had risen and were divesting themselves in leisurely fashion of a most complicated arrangement of motor coats and veils.

From these swathing disguises there first emerged, as if from a chrysalis, a black-clad, distinguished-looking young woman whom I had never seen before. However, it was the second figure, the one in the rosy veils and the tan mantle, that was exciting me. Off came her wrappings, and I saw a girl in a white gown and a flowered hat - the loveliest girl on earth.

I did not stand on the order of my going. I rocked perilously, and my crutches made a furious clatter, but I was outside in a truly infinitesimal space of time. Yes; there they were, chatting with Dunny, who had hurried to meet them. And at sight of me the Firefly of France ran forward with hands extended, greeting me as if I were his oldest friend, his brother, his dearest comrade in arms.

I took his hands and I pressed them with what show of warmth I could summon. It was as peasant as a bit of torture, but it had to be gone through. Then I stared past him toward the ladies, who were coming up with Dunny; and except for that girl in white, I saw nothing in all the world.

"Monsieur," the duke was saying, "I pay you my first visit. Only my weakness has prevented me from sooner welcoming to Raincy-la-Tour so honored a guest."

He turned to the lady who stood beside Miss Falconer, a slender, dark-eyed, gracious young woman wearing a simple black gown and a black hat and a string of pearls.

"Here is another," said the Firefly, "who has come to welcome you. Oh, yes, Monsieur, you must know, and you must count henceforth as your friends in any need, even to the death, all those who bear the name of Raincy-la-Tour. Permit that I present you to my wife, who is of your country."

"Jean's wife is my sister, Mr. Bayne," Miss Falconer said.

CHAPTER XXVI

AN UNEXPECTED VISIT

I don't know what they thought of me, probably that I was crazy. For a good minute, a long sixty seconds, I simply stood and stared. The duke's blue uniform, his wife's black-gowned figure, and the white, radiant blur that was Miss Falconer revolved about me in spinning, starry circles. I gasped, put out a hand, fortunately encountered Dunny's shoulder, and, leaning heavily on that perplexed person, at last got back my intelligence and my breath.

"Won't you shake hands with me, Mr. Bayne?" smiled the Duchess of Raincy-la-Tour.

I was virtually sane again.

"I do hope," I said, "that you will forgive me. Not that I see the slightest reason why you should, I am sure. Life is too short to wipe out such a bad impression. I know how you'll remember me all your days; as an idiot with a head done up in layers of toweling, wobbling on two crutches and gaping at you like a fish."

But the duchess was still holding my hand in both of hers and smiling up at me from a pair of great, dark, tender eyes, the loveliest pair of eyes in the world, bar one. No, bar none, to be quite fair. The Firefly's wife, most people would have said, was more beautiful than her sister; but then, beauty is what pleases you, as some wise man remarked long ago.

"I don't believe, Mr. Bayne," she was saying gently, "that I shall ever remember you in any unpleasant way. You see, I know about those bandages, and I know why you need those crutches. Even if you were vain, you wouldn't mind the things I think of you - not at all."

I lack any clear recollection of the quarter of an hour that followed. I know that we talked and laughed and were very friendly and very cheerful, and that Dunny's eyes, as they studied me, began to hold a gleam of intelligence, as if he were guessing something about the reasons for my former black despondency. I recall that the duke's hand was on my shoulder, and that - odd how one's attitude can change! - I liked to feel it. We were going to be great friends, tremendous pals, I suspected. And every time I looked at the duchess she seemed lovelier, more gracious; she was the very wife I would have chosen for such a corking chap.

This, however, was by the way. None of it really mattered. While I paid compliments and supplied details as to my convalescence and answered Dunny's chaffing, I saw only one member of the party, the girl in white. She was rather silent; she gave me only fugitive glances. But she wasn't engaged, at least not to the Firefly. Hurrah!

What an agonizing, heart-rending, utterly unnecessary experience I had endured, now that I thought of it! I had jumped to conclusions with the agility of a kangaroo. He had kissed her; she had allowed it. Did that prove that he was her fiance? He might have been anything - her cousin or an old friend of her childhood, or her sister's husband's nephew. But brother-in-law was best of all, not too remote or yet too close. In that relationship, I decided, he was ideal.

By this time I was wondering how long we were to stand here exchanging ideas and persiflage, an animated group of five. The duke and duchess were charming, but I had had enough of them; I could have spared even good old Dunny; what I wanted, and wanted frantically, was a tete-a-tete; just Esme Falconer and myself. When I saw two automobiles, packed imposingly with uniformed figures, speed up the drive to the chateau, hope stirred in me. With suppressed joy, - I trust it was suppressed, - I heard the duke exclaim that this was General Le Cazeau, due to visit the hospital with his staff and greet the wounded and bestow on certain lucky beings the reward of their valor in the shape of medals of war. Obviously, it would have been inexcusable for the master and mistress of Raincy-la-Tour to ignore a visitor so distinguished. I made no protest whatever as they turned to go.

"But, Miss Falconer," I implored fervently, "you won't desert me, will you? Pity a poor *blesse* that no general cares two straws to see!"

She smiled, an omen that encouraged me to send Dunny a look of meaning; but my guardian, bless him, had grasped the situation; he was already gone.

Down by the water among the trees there was a marble

bench, and with one accord we turned our steps that way. I emphasized my game leg shamelessly; I positively flourished my crutches. My battle scars, I guessed from the girl's kind eyes, appealed to her compassion, and as soon as I suspected this I thanked my stars for that German shell.

"Isn't there anything," she said as we sat down, "that you want to ask me? I think I should be curious if I were you. After all we have done together there isn't much beyond my name that you know of me, and you knew that in Jersey City the night the *Re d'Italia* sailed."

I shook my head.

"There is just one thing I wanted to know," I answered cryptically, "and I learned that when your brother-in-law presented me to his wife. Still, there is nothing on earth you can tell me that I shan't be glad to listen to. Say the multiplication table if you like, or recite cook-book recipes. Anything - if you'll only stay!"

Little golden flickers of sunshine came stealing through the branches, dancing, as the girl talked, on her gown and in her hair. I looked more than I listened. I had been starved for a sight of her. And my eyes must have told my thoughts; for a flush crept into her cheeks, and her lashes fluttered, and she looked not at me, but across the swan-dotted lake toward the towers of Raincy-la-Tour.

After all there was little that I had not guessed already; but each detail held its magic, because it was she who spoke. If she had said "I like oranges and lemons," the statement would have held me spellbound. I sat raptly gazing while she told me of herself and her sister Enid; of their life, after the death of their parents, with an aunt whose home was in Pittsburgh, of their travels; and of a winter at Nice, four years ago, when the blue of the skies and seas and the whiteness of the sands and the green of the palms had all seemed created to frame the meeting and the love affair of Enid Falconer and the young nobleman who was now known to the world as the Firefly of France.

Their marriage had proved an ideal one, as happy as it was brilliant. Esme, thereafter had spent half her time in Europe with her sister, half in America with her aunt, who was growing old. Then had come the war. At first it had covered the duke with laurels. But a certain dark day had brought a cable from the duchess, telling of his disappearance and the suspicion that surrounded it; and Esme, despite her aunt's entreaties, had promptly taken passage on the next ship that sailed.

"I had meant to go within a month, as a Red Cross nurse," she told me. "I had my passport, and I had taken a course. Well, I came on to New York and spent the night there. Aunt Alice telegraphed to her lawyer, the dearest, primmest old fellow, and he dined with me, protesting all the time against my sailing. I saw you in the St. Ives restaurant. Did you see us?"

"Let me think." I pretended to rack my brains. "I believe I do recall something, in a hazy sort of way. You had on a rose-colored gown that was distinctly wonderful, and when we tracked the German to the door of your room, you were wearing an evening coat, bright blue. But the main thing was your hair!" Here I became lyric. " An oak-leaf in the sunlight , Miss

Falconer! Threads of gold!"

But she ignored me, very properly, and shifted the scene from hotel to steamer, where Franz von Blenheim, in the guise of Van Blarcom, had given her a fright. As she exhibited her passport at the gangplank, he had read her name across her shoulder; then he had claimed acquaintance with her, a claim that she knew was false.

"And he wasn't impertinent. That was the worst of it," she faltered. "He did it - well - accusingly. I had known all along that any one who knew of Jean's marriage would recognize my name. And Jean was suspected, and the French are strict; if they were warned, they would not let me enter France; they would think I had come spying. I was afraid. Then, after dinner, I went on deck and found you standing by the railing reading that paper with its staring headlines about Jean."

"Of course!" I exclaimed. At last I fathomed that puzzling episode. "You thought the paper might speak of the duke's marriage, that it might mention your sister's name. In that case, if it stayed on board, it might be seen by the captain or by an officer, and they would guess who you were and warn the authorities when we got to shore."

"Yes. That was why I borrowed it. And I was right, I discovered; just at the end the account said that Jean had married an American, a Miss Enid Falconer, four years ago. Then I asked you to throw it overboard, Mr. Bayne; and you were wonderful. You must have thought I was mad, but you didn't flutter an eyelid or even smile. I have never forgotten - and I've never forgiven myself either. When I think of how the steward saw you and told the captain, and of how they searched your baggage that dreadful day -"

"It didn't matter a brass farden!" I hastened to assure her, for she had paused and was gazing at me, large-eyed and pale. "Don't think of that any more. Suppose we skip to Paris! Blenheim followed you there, hoping he was on the scent of the vanished papers; and when you arrived at the rue St.-Dominique, there was still no news of the duke."

"No news," she mourned; "not a word. And Enid was ill and hopeless; from the very first she had felt sure that Jean was dead. But I wouldn't admit it. I said we must try to find him. All the way over in the steamer I had been making a sort of plan.

"You see, one of the papers had described how the French had found Jean's airship lying in the forest of La Fay, as if he had abandoned it from choice. That was considered proof of his treason; but of course I knew that it wasn't. I remembered that the Marquis of Prezelay, Jean's cousin, had a castle on the forest outskirts; I had been to visit it with Jean and Enid. I wondered if he might be there.

"The more I thought of it, the likelier it seemed. If he had been wounded and had wanted to hide his papers, he would have remembered the castle and the secret panel in the wall. Even if he were - dead, which I wouldn't believe, it would clear his name if I found the proof of it. So I told Enid I would go to Prezelay."

I was resting my arms on my knees and groaning softly.

"Oh, Lord, oh, Lord!" I murmured, wishing I could stop my ears. When I thought of that brave venture of the girl's and its perils and what had nearly come of it I found myself shuddering; and yet I was growing prouder of her with every word.

"What comes next," she confessed, "is terrible. I can hardly believe it. As I look back, it seems to me that we were all a little mad. To get through the war zone to Prezelay I had to have certain papers; and I got them from an American girl, an old friend of Enid's and of mine, Marie Le Clair. The morning I arrived in Paris she came to say good-bye to Enid. She was acting as a Red Cross nurse, and they were sending her to the hospital at Carrefonds to take the first consignment of the great new remedy for burns and scars. Carrefonds is very near Prezelay. It all came to me in a moment. I told her how matters stood and how Enid was dying little by little, just for lack of any sure knowledge. She gave me the papers she had for herself and her chauffeur, Jacques Carton, and I used them for myself and for Georges, Jean's foster-brother, who was at home from the Front on leave and was staying in his old room at the house."

"Great Caesar's ghost!" I sputtered. "You didn't - you don't mean to say that - Why, good heavens, didn't you know -?"

Then I petered off into silence; words were too weak for my emotions. She had seen the risk of course, and so had the girl who had helped her; but with the incredible bravery of women, they had acted with open eyes.

"Yes," she faltered; "I told you I felt mad, looking back

at it. But Marie is safe now; Jean has worked for her, and his relatives and friends have helped, and the minister of war. It was the only way. Under my own name I could never have got leave to enter the war zone while Jean was missing and suspected - What is the matter, Mr. Bayne?" For once more I had groaned aloud.

"Simply," I cried stormily, "that I can't bear thinking of it! The idea of your taking risks, of your daring the police and the Germans - you who oughtn't to know what the word danger means! I tell you I can't stand it. Wasn't there some man to do it for you? Well, it's over now; and in the future - See here, Miss Falconer, I can't wait any longer. There is something I've got to say."

But I was not to say it yet, for, behold! just as my tongue was loosened, I became aware of a most distinguished galaxy approaching us round the lake. All save one of its members - Dunny, to be exact - were in uniform; and the personage in the lead, walking between my guardian and the duke of Raincy-la-Tour, was truly dazzling, being arrayed in a blue coat and spectacularly red trousers and wearing as a finishing touch a red cap freely braided with gold. Miss Falconer had risen.

"Why," she exclaimed, "it is General Le Cazeau!"

"Then confound General Le Cazeau!" was my inhospitably cry.

He was, I saw when he drew close, a person of stately dignity, as indeed the hero who had saved Merlancourt and broken that last furious, desperate, senseless onslaught of the Boches ought by rights to be. Perhaps his splendor made me nervous. At any rate, my conscience smote me. I remembered with sudden panic all my manifold transgressions, beginning with the hour when I had chucked reason overboard and had deliberately concealed a murdered man's body beneath a heap of straw.

"I believe," I gasped, "that this is an informal court martial. Nobody could do the things I have done and be allowed to live. Still, I don't see why they cured me if they were going to hang or shoot me."

I struggled up with the help of my crutches and stood waiting my doom.

The group had paused before us, and presentations followed, throughout which the master of ceremonies was the Firefly of France. Then the gray-headed general fixed me with a keen, stern gaze rather like an eagle's.

"Your affair, Monsieur, has been of an irregularity," he said.

As with kaleidoscopic swiftness the details of my "affair" passed through my memory, it was only by an effort that I restrained an indecorous shout. He was correct. I could call to mind no single feature that had been "regular," from the thief who was not a thief and had flown out of my window like a conjurer, to the fight in Prezelay castle where I had vanquished four husky Germans, mostly by the aid of a wooden table, of all implements on earth.

" It is too true , *Monsieur le General* , " I assented

promptly. My humility seemed to soften him; he relaxed; he even approached a smile.

"Of an irregularity," he repeated. "But also it was of a gallantry. With a boldness and a resource and a scorn for danger that, permit me to say, mark your compatriots, you have unmasked and handed over to us one of our most dangerous foes. For such service as you have rendered France is never ungrateful. And, moreover, there have been friends to plead your cause and to plead it well."

As he ended he cast a glance at the Duke of Raincy-la-Tour and one at Dunny, whereupon I was enlightened as to the purpose of my guardian's three trips to Paris the preceding week. I believe I have said before that Dunny knows every one, everywhere; in fact, I have always felt that should circumstances conspire to make me temporarily adopt a life of crime, he could manage to pull such wires as would reinstate me in the public eye. But the general was stepping close to me.

"Monsieur," he was saying, "we are now allies, my country and the great nation of which you are a son. Very soon your troops are coming. You will fight on our soil, beneath your own banner. But your first blood was shed for France, your first wounds borne for her, Monsieur; and in gratitude she offers you this medal of her brave."

He was pinning something to my coat, a bronze-colored, cross-shaped something, a decoration that swung proudly from a ribbon of red and green. I knew it well; I had seen it on the breasts of generals, captains, simple poilus, all the picked flower of the

French nation. With a thrill I looked down upon it. It was the Cross of War.

Marion Polk Angellotti

CHAPTER XXVII

A THUNDERBOLT OF WAR

The great moment had arrived. General Le Cazeau and his staff were on their way back to Paris. The duke and duchess were at the chateau talking with the *blesses*; for the second time Dunny had tactfully disappeared. The approach of evening had spurred my faltering courage. As the first rosiness of sunset touched the skies beyond Raincy-la-Tour and lay across the water, I sat at the side of the only girl in the world and poured out my plea.

"It isn't fair, you know," I mourned. "I've only a few minutes. I shouldn't wonder if we heard your car honking for you in half an hour. To make a girl like you look at a man like me would take days of eloquence, and, besides, who would think of marrying any one with his head bound up Turkish fashion as mine is now?"

She laughed, and at the silvery sound of it I plucked up a hint of courage; for surely, I thought, she wasn't cruel enough to make game of me as she turned me down. Still, I couldn't really hope. She was too wonderful, and my courtship had been too inadequate. Despondent, arms on my knees, I harped upon the same string.

"I've never had a chance to show you," I lamented, "that I am civilized; that I know how to take care of you and put cushions behind you and slide footstools under your feet, and - er - all that. We've been too busy eluding Germans and racing through forbidden zones and rescuing papers from behind secret panels, for me to wait on you. Good heavens! To think how I've done my duty by a hundred girls I shouldn't know from Eve if they happened along this moment! And I've never even sent you a box of *marrons glaces* or flowers."

She shot a fleeting glance at me.

"No," she agreed, "you haven't! If you don't mind my saying so, I think they would have been out of place. At Bleau, for instance, and at Prezelay I hadn't much time for eating bonbons; but after all you did me one or two more practical services, Mr. Bayne."

"Nothing," I maintained, my gloom unabated, "that amounted to a row of pins. Though I might have shone, I'll admit; I can see that, looking back. The opportunity was there, but the man was lacking. I might have been a real movie hero, cool, resourceful, dependable, clear-sighted, a tower of strength; and what I did was to muddle things up hopelessly and waste time in suspecting you and seize every opportunity of trusting people who positively spread their guilt before my eyes."

"I don't know." She was looking at the lake, not at me, and she was smiling. "There were one or two little matters that have slipped your mind, perhaps. Take the very first night we met, when you tracked your thief to my room and wouldn't let the hotel people come in to search it. Don't you think, on the whole, that you were rather kind?"

"I couldn't have driven them in," I declared stubbornly, "with a pitchfork. I couldn't have persuaded them to make a search if I had prayed them on my bended knees. Their one idea was to help the fellow in what the best criminal circles call a getaway; and when I think how I must have been wool-gathering, not to guess -"

"Well, even so," - Miss Falconer was still smiling - "weren't you very nice on the steamer? About the extra, I mean. And at Gibraltar, too, when they asked you what you had thrown overboard - do you remember how you kept silent and never even glanced my way?"

"No," I groaned, "I don't; but I remember our trip to Paris. I remember marching you into the wagon-restaurant like a hand-cuffed criminal, and sitting you down at a table, and bullying you like a Russian czar. I gave you three days to leave France. Have you forgotten? I haven't. The one thing I omitted - and I don't see how I missed it - was to call the gendarmes there at Modane and denounce you to them. It's more than kind of you to glide over my imbecilities; I appreciate it. But when I think of that evening I want a nice, deep, dark dungeon, somewhere underground, to hide."

"I think," she murmured consolingly, "that you made amends to me later." Her face was averted, but I could see a distracting dimple in her cheek. "You mustn't forget that I haven't been perfect, either. When you followed me to Bleau, and I came down the stairs and saw you , I misunderstood the situation entirely and was as unpleasant as I could be."

"Naturally," I acquiesced with dark meaning. "How could you have understood it? How could any human being have fathomed the mental processes that sent me there? I only wonder that instead of giving me what-for, you didn't murder me. Any United States jury would have acquitted you with the highest praise."

She turned upon me, flushed and spirited.

"Mr. Bayne, you are incorrigible! Why will you insist on belittling everything that you have done? I suppose you will claim next that you didn't risk imprisonment or death every minute of a whole day, just to help me, and that at Prezelay you didn't fight like a - a - yes, like a paladin! - to save me from being tortured by Herr von Blenheim and his men!"

I started up and then sank back.

"As a special favor," I begged her, "would you mind not mentioning that last phase of the affair? When you do, I go berserker; I'm a crazy man, seeing red; I'm honestly not responsible. It was when our friend Blenheim developed those plans of his that I swore in my soul I'd get him; and I thank the Lord that I did and that he'll never trouble you or any other woman again.

"Still, Miss Falconer, what does all that amount to? Any man would have helped you, wouldn't he? A nice sort of fellow I should have been to do any less! Whereas for a girl like you I ought to have accomplished miracles. I ought to have made the sun stop moving, or got you the stars to play with, or whisked the moon out of the skies."

She was laughing again.

"Dear me!" she exclaimed. "What fervor! Can this be my Mr. Bayne, the Mr. Bayne of our adventure, who never turned a hair no matter what mad things happened, and who was always so correct and conventional and so immaculately dressed, and so - "

"Stodgy! Say it!" I cried with utter recklessness. "I know I was; Dunny told me so that evening at the St. Ives. Have as many cracks at me as you like. I was getting fat; I was beginning to think that the most important thing in the universe was dinner. Well, I'm not stodgy any longer, Esme Falconer; you've reformed me. But of all the men in all the ages who were ever desperately, consumedly, imbecilely in love -"

In the distance two figures were strolling toward the blue car, the duke and the duchess. When they reached it, the Firefly cast a glance in our direction and sounded a warning, most unwelcome honk upon the horn. They were going, stony-hearted creatures that they were! They were taking Esme back to Paris. At the thought I abandoned my last pretense at self-command.

"Esme, dearest," I implored, "do you think you could put up with me? Could you marry me when I've done my part over here - or even sooner - right away? A dozen better men may love you, but mine is a special brand of love - unique, incomparable! Are you going to have me - or shall I jump into the lake?"

The sunset light was in her hair and in the gray, starry eyes she turned to me - those eyes that, because their lashes were so long and crinkled so maddeningly, were only half revealed. Her lips curved in a fleeting smile.

"Oh, you dear, blind, silly man! Do you think any girl could help loving you - after all that has happened to you and me?" she whispered.

Then I caught her to me; and despite my crutches and my bandaged head and that atrocious horn in the distance honking the signal for our parting, I was the happiest being in France - or in the world.

"I knew all along it was a dream, and it is! Such things don't really happen. No such luck!" I cried.

www.ingramcontent.com/pod-product-compliance
Lightning Source LLC
Chambersburg PA
CBHW030134180626
46812CB00002B/679